DEMON

Book One of Archive of the God Eater

Editor: Sarah Chorn

Cover Art: Eshpur

Cover Design: STK• Kreations

www.robjhayes.co.uk

DEMON

ARCHIVE OF THE GOD EATER BOOK 1

THE GOD EATER SAGA

ROB J. HAYES

A NOTE FROM THE AUTHOR

Time for a little info on format. DEMON is book 1 of the Archive of the God Eater trilogy, and also part of the larger God Eater Saga which will consist of 9 books.

The God Eater Saga is a trilogy of trilogies being written and released concurrently. That means I wrote all 3 book 1s at the same time and I'm releasing them together. I've also started writing all 3 book 2s and will be releasing them together as well. I know, it's a strange way to do things, but bear with me.

Writing and releasing the saga this way allows me to weave mysteries, reveals, world building, and character development across the 9 books and across 3000 years of in world history. I felt it was important to do it this way because many of the characters in God Eater are immortals and have been alive a LONG time.

But fear not! Each trilogy is designed to work on its own as well. If you just want to read Dien's trilogy (ARCHIVE OF THE GOD EATER), that's fine, you'll get all the pertinent information you need within those pages. But if you choose to read the full saga (AGE OF THE GOD EATER, ANNALS OF THE GOD EATER, ARCHIVE OF THE GOD EATER), you'll get a much deeper understanding of the world and the story. And there may be some reveals in the past that shine a new light on events in the present.

For ease of understanding when all 3 trilogies take place, here's a handy little summary:

<u>Age of the God Eater</u> (main series)
    Herald (book 1)

<u>Annals of the God Eater</u> (set 1000 years before Herald)
    Deathless (book 1)

<u>Archive of the God Eater</u> (set 3000 years before Herald)
    Demon (book 1)

I know it all sounds a little confusing. Believe me, it was certainly a headache keeping it all straight in my head. But I can assure you it will all make sense in the end.

THANK YOU for reading, and I do hope you check out all 3 trilogies to get the best understanding of the world.

Rob

CHAPTER I

The stars were bright the night Dien's world ended.

Someone thumped the front door hard enough Dien thought it might be a bear. The beasts tracked through the forest sometimes, looking for easy prey, but they never broke into homes. Much more likely to be a demon.

The thump sounded three more times in quick succession. Not a demon, then. Dien might never have seen one of the monsters and, Moon and Sun willing, she never would, but the stories were quite certain on one thing. Demons didn't knock.

She left the dough she was kneading and wiped floury hands on her apron, then snuck towards the front door. She could hear her parents stirring from their room. Her ma whispered something sharp. Her da sighed.

Dien reached the door to their little wooden hovel just as whoever was outside thumped on it again, nearly making Dien jump out of her apron.

"Unter Hostain, you cheatin' sack of cat guts, git your carcass out here or I'll burn your hut to the loam with you inside, I will."

That seemed like an impotent threat and no mistake; no one would risk a fire these days and especially not at night, no matter how deep in the forest they were.

Their little cabin was sturdily built, far more so than most of the other homes in the scattered forest village. Her da had made sure of it. But next to the door one of the planks of wood had warped just a little, enough to create the smallest of gaps. Her da had nailed a sliver of wood over it and that sliver could be twisted aside to reveal the gap once more. Dien pressed in close to the wall, twisted the splinter of wood, and peered out into the brightening morning.

Harsh yellow light blazed back at her and she had to blink away the brightness. Whoever was outside *had* brought a torch with them. At night! It was madness. Everyone knew you never risked a fire at night. Better to huddle in the freezing cold, whole families piled under a single blanket than light a fire. Better to stumble blindly in the dark, as like to trip over your own feet as find the path than risk a flame. Fires in the night brought demons, everyone said so. Everyone agreed. No flames, no fires, no torches. Never at night and not even during the day when smoke could rise past the canopy.

Dien squinted against the light, looking away from it. She saw three figures outside, all men she knew. There was Iger Brane, the village brewer and drunk both, holding the torch with his one good hand and his club hand nestled against his chest. Next to him stood Metwit Pa, his hair lip and wild eyes making him look like a rabid beaver. She couldn't quite see the man standing in front of their door, but she recognised his voice now. He was Donnel Ocha, the Adjudicator's eldest son and soon to take the position once his ancient father breathed his last, which everyone said would be passing soon. Though everyone had been saying the same for well over a year now.

Donnel thumped on the door three more times. "Last chance, Hostain. This den ain't so sturdy I can't break it down."

The floorboards creaked behind her and Dien spun to find her da lumbering out of her parents' room. He had his oldest shirt on, the one with all the rips and tears he only wore to cut wood these days and pulled on his workday britches. He filled the corridor, but then he had built it so it was just wide enough for his broad shoulders. He had built every bit of their little home, dug the foundations, laid every board, hammered every nail. He yawned and stepped forward, already waving at Dien out of the way.

Dien stepped in front of her da and spread her arms out wide as if she could stop him. She wasn't as tall as her da, nor nearly so broad. Her ma said she had the Hostain shoulders though and the Hostains were all big. Sometimes her ma despaired about that, said Dien was almost a woman grown now and soon she'd have to find a husband, and that would be hard and harder once she grew into her shoulders so she better start looking soon. Her da always laughed at that and said any man who wanted to tame his little forge spark better be ready for the inferno she'd become. He often talked about forges, though Dien had never seen one. No one had. They couldn't risk them.

"They mean harm," Dien whispered as her da came close.

"Anger is a rotten log, little bug. Strong on the outside, but when you split it, you find nothing but weak fear within." He smiled down at her, looking almost like a bear himself in the near darkness of their cabin. "A rotten log has many uses, but you can never build with it."

With a casual strength, he placed his hands on her shoulders and steered her gently aside, then strode towards the door just as it thumped again.

"I hear you in there, Hostain. Out now!"

Her da paused and glanced to the side. The door to his tool cupboard was open. His axe and hammers, all the tools of his trade, hung in their cherished places on the wall, including the big hammer he never used. Sometimes Dien caught her ma glaring at those tools when da wasn't around. She asked why once and her ma had cried and said that cursed hammer hadn't been forged to build and she wished he'd be rid of it.

Her da reached out and slowly closed the door to the tool cupboard, then set his broad shoulders, twisted the locks, and threw open the door to the three men outside.

"Sun and Moons, Donnel Ocha," her da said as he stepped out of their home into the crisp morning. The Adjudicator's son backed up quickly, giving ground before his advance. "You lit a torch at night? Are you mad?"

"You're a cheatin' toad, Unter Hostain, and I'll have retribution for it, I will." With the torch flickering outside, casting its dangerous orange light all around, Dien could see Donnel's fist clenched by his side.

Dien took a step towards the door and was pulled short by her ma gripping her hand. She was still wearing her nightshirt, too large around the hips but pulled in by a fraying length of rope, and her raven hair was a wild tangle about her round face. Dien sometimes envied her ma's hair. She'd inherited her burnt sand skin, but she'd got her da's dull oaken hair.

Her ma shook her head. "Your father will deal with it, Dien."

Dien relented and let her ma pull her back a step, but she turned and stared out the open doorway.

"You want to tell me what this is about, Donnel?" her da said. "And I'll see about answering for it."

Donnel Ocha shuffled a step. The two men behind him spread out as if to flank her da in his own doorway.

"Act like you don't know?" Donnel snarled. "Call your work sound? Shoddy. Ill made, I say." He spat on the floor. "Wardrobe you made fell apart. Collapsed on my Shilly and almost crushed her. She can't walk no more. Broke foot, so Arnut says."

Arnut Poll was also known as The Knife, though never to his face. He was the village healer, or as close to one as they had, but everyone knew his skills with a blade weren't meant for healing. Helena said he was as bad as a demon himself, all leering grins and wandering hands.

"If Arnut says so, it's so," her da said, nodding. "Knows his trade."

"Better than you, for certain," Donnel hissed. "I demand reparations." He shifted and Dien saw Iger and Metwit closing in.

Her da glanced back into the house, his dark gaze sweeping over Dien before finding her ma. Then he turned back to Donnel, and took a heavy step forward, out of the cabin and onto the packed earth of the forest.

"It's the nails, Donnel. The lack of, to be exact. Can't make nails without a forge. Can't risk a forge for the same reason young Iger here should know better than lighting a torch. Put it out, lad. You'll signal the demons right to us."

Donnel raised his hand and poked a finger against her da's chest. He didn't budge. "It ain't fire gonna call the demons. It's cheating shits like you. Think I don't know you, Unter Hostain? Think I don't know the past you're runnin' from?"

Her da sighed again. "It's the lack of nails, Donnel. Gotta use dowels instead. They slot nicely, hold it together just fine. But too much wear will loosen them some and then..."

"My fault now, is it?" Donnel shouted.

"Voice down, lad," her da warned. "Sound travels at night."

"Shilly's fault, is it?" Donnel barrelled on. "Pulled the wardrobe down on herself, did she?"

Her da raised his hands, not threatening, just placating. "I'm not saying that, Donnel. I'll come repair the break at first light. Make it good as new."

"And what about my Shilly? Broke foot, so Arnut says. Can't walk. Can't tend chicks, fetch water. Can't do nothin' but bitch at me. What'll you do about her, Unter Hostain? Cheating pile of shit, what'll you do about her?"

"Any grievance you got should be brought to the Adjudicator, Donnel," her da' said. "That ain't you yet."

Donnel stopped shifting about and went still. Dien sensed a dangerous change in the air. Her ma's hand tightened on her arm.

"Yet," Donnel said. He lurched forward and Dien's da grunted as a fist connected with his gut, but still, he didn't move.

"Don't want to do this, Donnel," her da growled.

They closed on him from three sides like wolves hunting deer. Metwit had a wooden club and smashed it into her da's leg. He staggered, went down to his knees, and then they were all there, raining punches and kicks down on him. Her da raised his arms, protecting his head, but he didn't fight back. Iger dropped his torch so he could use his good hand to punch. His fist caught her da's ear and he fell to the floor under a flurry of thuds and grunts.

Dien tried to go to him, even knowing she couldn't help. Her ma kept hold of her, pulling on Dien to hold her back. Dien's eyes fell to the torch Iger had dropped. It was sputtering, sizzling. The flames were licking at the wooden wall of their cabin, blackening it. If it started burning, they wouldn't be able to stop it. The fire would spread and consume their home. And worse, the smoke would call the demons to them. The whole village would pay.

Her blood boiled. Like the fires from the torch were coursing through her veins. Burning. Tight and painful and demanding she do something. Dien wrenched free of her ma and ran for the door. She slipped around the melee, shoving her broad shoulder against Iger and sending him stumbling. She snatched the torch from the ground before the cabin wall could catch light, then turned to face her da's attackers, torch held in trembling hands.

"Get away from him!" Dien shouted.

Donnel looked up, then kicked her da in the ribs again. Metwit stopped his assault and stepped around the struggle, heading for her. Iger snarled and launched himself at her, reaching with his one good hand. Dien staggered back, swung the torch with both hands. The fiery end smacked into Iger's chest, crashing against his club hand. He screamed, fell back, his shirt sizzling.

"Stupid bitch!" Metwit snarled and reached for her.

Dien swung for him, too, but Metwit grabbed the torch halfway up the haft, halting the swing. The back of his hand smashed into Dien's face. She fell, clutching at her throbbing cheek, hit the wall, and moaned, tears already flooding her eyes. Metwit had the torch in his hand now and advanced on her.

Donnel stumbled away as if pushed, almost fell. Dien's da rose like a startled raven taking flight, sudden and dark as beating wings. "Don't you dare touch her," he rumbled, taking a step forward and towering over Metwit. The smaller man backed away, wild eyes darting about. "You'll leave my family out of this, Donnel."

Dien's face throbbed with her racing heart. The fire had gone out of her blood now, replaced by cold shock and sullen anger. She pressed a hand against her cheek where Metwit had hit her and it was already feeling swollen. Nobody had ever hit her before. She'd seen her father take punches many times, sometimes in anger and others in jest. It never seemed to faze him, but it hurt so much.

Donnel and the others ran then, disappearing into the forest, back to their homes. Her da watched them go. The sun was rising, brightening the sky so some of the other scattered cabins were now visible. Yet all the shutters were closed. If any of the nearby villagers had heard the scuffle, none came to investigate.

Her da knelt before her and peeled Dien's hand away from her cheek. He sighed. "That's gonna be a nasty bruise, little bug." He stood and gently pulled Dien to her feet. Then turned and headed inside.

Dien's ma was sprawled on the floor where Dien had shoved her, sobbing quietly. Her da went to her and checked her over too, then pulled her to her feet.

"Why?" Dien asked from the doorway, staring at her parents. "Why didn't you fight back?"

Her da glanced over his shoulder at her and winced. "A man must face up to the consequences of his actions. Accept them. Own them."

"But you didn't do anything wrong," Dien said. She didn't understand. "You said yourself, you can't make nails. You made the wardrobe as sturdy as you could but..."

Her da shook his head. "That wasn't about a wardrobe, little bug. And I've done plenty wrong. Consequences are like your shadow. Sometimes they're before you, and sometimes behind, but they're always there. You can never escape your shadow, no matter how far you try to run from it."

The bright blue of a dazzling morning sky was peeking through the canopy of leaves as Dien finally left the house, dough ready for baking in hand. She was late and her face throbbed where Metwit had hit her. Still, she had jobs to do and sulking in the hut wouldn't accomplish any of them.

The village was already a'bustle. Opposite the village hall, the largest building in the village by far, huntsmen and woodsmen assembled their teams, ready to lope off into the deep forest. Women were busy carrying washing or dough or fetching water.

In the centre of the village square, Panyet worked the well, his muscled shoulders straining as he hauled up bucket after bucket. Dien watched him as she passed. He was a rangy young man with earthy skin and a dark tangle of hair that seemed forever fallen in front of his eyes. She thought him handsome, not that he'd ever looked at her. She hurried past with only a single glance back at him.

There was already a gaggle of villagers waiting to speak with the Adjudicator: old Swiff, miss Trudie, and Enna Rusk. Dien wandered if her da would seek an audience and bring some justice down on Donnel. But she knew he wouldn't. He'd just fix Donnel's broken cupboard and say no more of the matter. It was his way.

The village had just the one oven and it was designed so no smoke would escape. It was built into the earth, the fire placed on top of the oven itself. Wet smothering sheets were stretched above the fire to catch any smoke, and a layer of leaves atop of them. Added to that, the oven was set up where the trees were thickest so the leaves above would catch any smoke that did escape the damp sheets. Aren Tivers worked it, all day, every day and most villagers said he was more sweat than man because of it. But none said it to his face because he was too useful to anger. He tended the fire, kept the smothering sheets wet, and used his paddle to slot the dough in and take it out when it was baked. The village had a kiln as well, for firing the clay to make the pottery they needed, but that was kept underground in a cave to the west. The smoke there had to travel so far to reach the surface, it was almost entirely dissipated by the time it did.

Helena was already at the oven, waiting her turn, and waved Dien to join her. "Over here," she said. "Just cut in."

"Hey!" Luci Yolk said, standing behind Helena.

"Oh stuff it, Luci," Helena said. "Dien would do the same for you."

Luci grumbled something and wrung her hands but didn't argue. "What happened to your face?"

Dien decided the gossip was too juicy to hold in. "Donnel Ocha and his cronies tried to break down our door last night. Threatened to burn the cabin. They had a torch and everything."

Luci gasped. Helena narrowed her eyes. Her da was the village fire-keeper. No one else was supposed to so much as coax a flame. It was said Rankin Tressel knew more about fire than the sun itself, which also explained his lack of eyebrows.

Dien traced a light hand across her black eye. "They attacked my da and that shit-headed fool Metwit gave me this when I went to stop the torch from catching anything else alight."

"Does it hurt?" Luci asked.

Dien shook her head. "Not much." As if in answer to her lie, her cheek pulsed a dull ache.

"You just rescued the torch? And he hit you?"

Dien shrugged. "I might have smacked Iger Brane with the fiery end first."

"Of course you did." Helena grinned. "He's lucky I wasn't there or he'd have found it shoved up his arse." They all had a giggle at that, even Luci, though she covered her mouth to hide it.

They reached the front of the queue and Aren Tivers held out his paddle while each of them placed their balls of dough on it, then he slid them into the oven and grunted for them to leave. Aren never said much that wasn't a manly grunt. It made him beyond tedious.

With their bread in the oven, they had a quarter of a sun before the dough was baked and had plenty of other jobs to be about. Life was a routine that would never be broken except in special occasions such as a marriage or a death, and the village of Berrywhistle hadn't had either for a while now, though everyone said there should be a marriage soon. They often looked at Dien when they said it, though more often they were looking at Luci.

They skipped along to the mill, Dien and Helena hand in hand, Luci trailing a few steps behind as she always did. Helena was wearing her burgundy dress today and that meant it was Hornsday. She always wore the burgundy when traders came to visit the village. She said it contrasted wonderfully with her pale skin, which was true, and that she was trying to look pretty, to catch the eye of some trader who would marry her and take her away from the village because she was so bored with looking at the same tired faces day in and out. Rarely a day went by when Helena didn't talk about some far distant land like it was the last, juiciest apple in the basket.

The mill was where they ground the flour to make dough each day and there were already six other women hard at work, grinding pestle and mortar together.

Dien sat at her own mortar, hitched up her shift a little and gripped the stone basin with her knees. She scooped up a handful of dried bugs and tossed them in, then hefted the pestle in both hands and started working it round and round in a monotonous motion.

"Today's the day," Helena said through gritted teeth as she worked.

"You think?" Dien asked.

"It has to be. I'm so sick of all of this. So bored of grinding bugs and still finding the odd leg in my bread, caught between my teeth. Urgh, it's horrible."

"That's because you don't grind them enough," Luci added helpfully.

Helena scowled at the smaller girl, but the effort of working the pestle soon demanded her attention again. "Today, the traders from Lowfields and the Ice Plains come. So, I'm going to look extra appealing and one of them is going to marry me and rescue me from all of this. You'll see."

"You want to live on the Ice Plains?" Dien asked. She was already sweating from the effort of grinding the pestle and her cheek throbbed harder with the heat.

"Why not?"

"It's cold." Winters could get frosty in the forest, too, but it was nothing compared to the Ice Plains where the sea froze beneath a person's feet and the wind howled louder than any demon. "You hate the cold, Helena. And all the ice walkers eat is fish."

Helena grunted as she grabbed another handful of bugs. "I don't hate the cold that much," she said sulkily. "And I might like fish. Better than bug bread, anyway. Don't you want to leave, Dien? Don't you want someone to take you away from the drudgery?"

Dien thought about it for a moment and smiled despite the stiffness of her cheek. She shook her head. "I want my da to teach me his work. I want to learn how to build things."

Helena laughed as she scooped up another handful of bugs and tossed them into her mortar. "And you think *I'm* dreaming. Carpentry is men's work, Dien."

"Doesn't have to be. Trader just a few Hornsdays back said women in Black Crag work stone. Why not wood as well?"

"Oh, so you won't go to the Ice Plains because you don't like fish, but you'll cross the Burning Lands all the way to get to desolate Black Crag? You know they eat lizard eggs there? Maybe Enna Rusk is right and you are as crazy as your da."

Enna Rusk could shove all her many opinions up her nose for all Dien cared. She never could figure out why the older woman disliked her so, but Enna never passed up a chance to belittle Dien.

"You can't go to Black Crag," Luci said quietly from where she was labouring over her pestle. She paused when she realised Dien and Helena were staring at her. "You haven't heard? It's gone. Demons took it."

There didn't seem much to say to that. They all knew Black Crag was a long, long way to the east and the demons were pushing out further each year, claiming more land, taking more people. Everyone said the only reason they weren't demon thralls already was because the monsters spent as much time fighting each other as they did raiding human lands.

Dien scooped up another handful of bugs and sprinkled them into the growing pile of flour. She started grinding in silence. You couldn't fight demons; they were too strong. You couldn't run from them because they were too fast, many of them running on four legs instead of two. All they could do was hide. That was why people were scattered as they were, living in small villages, cowering in forests, in caves, on sheets of ice that stretched on forever and froze a person's bones in their bodies. All they could do was hide, everyone said so. It was just how things were.

After they were done grinding flour for tomorrow's dough, they collected their baked bread from the oven. Dien saw Metwit stroll past while she was waiting for her turn. He grinned at her, stroked his cheek, and blew her a kiss. She glared back as furiously as she could. The sour arse simply laughed and walked on.

Dien collected her bread rolls and took them back home. Her da would be ready for food and that had been her job for a handful of years now. Her ma spent most of her time in the gardens these days, helping Yona Yolk grow the herbs she needed for her work. Luci's ma was the village herbalist, which gave her about as much say in matters of healing as Arnut Poll, though most people went to Yona if she was about on account of her more pleasant demeanour.

Dien took her da's food out back to where he liked to work. He had a collection of hard wood planks leaning up against the wall of the cabin and another laid out on his workbench. Dien sat and watched him for a while, chewing on a slice of bug bread.

"What are you making?" she asked.

Her da looked up and scratched at his chin. His calloused hands were already dusty. "A wardrobe."

"What?" Dien nearly shouted. "For Donnel Ocha? After what he did, you should build him a coffin."

Her da smiled, took a bite of dried venison, and turned back to the plank of wood on his bench. He laid another stick on top and fished a wedge of charcoal from his pouch. "Donnel might be a selfish goat, but show me a young man who ain't. Or an old man who weren't just so in his younger days. Besides, it's not about him. Something I built fell apart, injured a young woman. I have enough pride left that I can't let that stand.

"Pride is a tool like any other, little bug. In the wrong hands, it can be a terrible thing. But it can also be used to inspire good in people. If you can retain enough pride to do the right thing, even in the face of scorn and ridicule, you can inspire that same pride in others."

"Because you shame them into it?" Dien asked.

Her da sighed. "Sometimes. Shame is another tool. But no. It's because you remind them of their own pride, and what it means to be human. That's what unites us all, in the end."

"Can you teach me?" Dien said before doubt could still her tongue.

Her da grinned through his beard. "To be human? Nah. You're a little bug."

She rolled her eyes at him. "To work wood. To build things."

"Oh that?" He laughed. "I can teach you that. First lesson: what's the most important tool a woodworker has?"

Dien considered the question. She glanced over to the cabin wall where her da had hung his axe, hammers, and chisels. They were all metal, forged proper. A fortune given no one could work a forge anymore without the smoke signalling to demons. Still, she sensed a trap. It was too easy to pick the axe or hammer. And hadn't he just been saying that pride was a tool? He was staring at her, chewing on bread, and waiting for her answer.

Dien raised her hand and tapped a single finger against her head. "Your mind."

Her da swallowed and nodded. "Smart little bug. But still wrong." He grabbed the long stick he'd laid on the wooden plank and tossed it to her. "That is the most important tool a wood worker has."

Dien caught the stick and looked at it, then sighed. "Wood. Wood is the most important tool."

"Wrong again. Look more closely."

She frowned and lifted the stick to stare at it. It was long and straight, a single length of wood. Pine, she thought. It was notched in multiple places along its length and every single notch was blackened by charcoal.

"It's a measuring stick."

"Exactly that. Our most important tool. Not just for wood workers, but for anyone looking to build. Doesn't matter whose measurements you use, so long as you keep them consistent. Otherwise, anything you try to build will be ill fitting and it will fall apart on the first test. Most of what I do is measuring, little bug. Remember that. Whether it's this plank of wood for a wardrobe, or a man threatening to burn down my home in the dead of night. Always measure before you act."

Her da spent an eighth of a sun teaching Dien to measure, then re-measure, then measure again. It would have been maddening but for the time spent by his side. She didn't even mind his awful jokes. But the day rolled on, and Dien's tasks were far from complete.

She spent a full fifth a sun with her mother on the sewing benches. It was customary for all the women of Berrywhistle to dedicate some time to sewing each day, keeping old dresses and shirts mended and wearable, darning socks. Dien hadn't a head for it and was as like to rip new holes in clothing as fix existing ones. And she had the compelling desire to burn every sock handed to her long before she stabbed her finger with a needle trying to patch it. Her mother had long ago realised this and gave Dien the child's task of whittling new needles instead. It was so simple and she'd been doing it long enough it was second nature now. Sitting around with children half her age, Dien took rabbit bones and scraped away at them with a bit of flint, shaving off layer after layer until the little bone ended in a fine point. The needles were fragile things and every woman broke one or two with each sewing session, but they had rabbit bones to spare, children to put to work, and so new needles aplenty.

After her tiresome shift with her mother. Dien met back up with Helena and Luci as they all collected their baskets and went out into the meadows.

There were some places in the forest where the trees did not grow. The Adjudicator, who also served as the educator for the village, claimed it was because the earth was not right for them. That trees needed strong soil to lay deep foundations and any stable colony, be it forest or human, needed solid foundations. Which might have held some truth, but everyone said the people who lived on the Ice Plains were always moving, and ice was a terrible place to lay foundations anyway, and yet live there people did. So, too, were the people of the Burning Lands unable to lay deep foundations because the land regularly burst into flames as black as night. And yet people lived there also, despite the fires.

Regardless, something stopped the trees from growing in the meadows, but grass grew thick and tall, and that made it the perfect place to harvest the bugs they needed for flour. So Dien, Helena, and Luci spent a full quarter of a sun foraging and filling their baskets with squirmers, jumpers, and crawlers.

Helena mostly collected the squirming kind, filling her basket with mealworms and snatchfly larva, because she didn't like breaking the legs of the jumping type. It was the only way to keep the little buggers inside the basket, but she had too kind a heart for it. So Dien traded squirmers for jumpers and saved her friend the pain by breaking the legs herself.

By the time they'd filled their baskets, the sun had dropped below the tree line and light was fleeing the world. Already the Caped Moon had risen, a pale sliver in the dark blue sky, almost translucent. The Bone Moon was rising too. It always promised to be a rowdy night whenever two or more moons shared the sky. Last time the Blood Moon rose with the Bone, a fight had broken out between handsome Panyet and Mayhew Tivers. Mayhew lost a finger in the scuffle and Panyet had taken a lashing across the back as punishment. He took it with only a grunt as acknowledgement, which Dien thought was incredibly manly.

The three girls hurried back through the forest towards the village. It wasn't that you couldn't navigate the endless trees at night, but it was a lot more difficult, and dangerous. Bears were rare, and never came into homes, but they prowled the forest all the same. And some people said there were worse things. Not demons, but monsters all the same. Enna Rusk said she'd seen something huge and scaly lumbering through the trees a few weeks back. But then, Dien had to admit that Enna Rusk said a lot of things and they rarely turned out to be worth listening to.

Luci struggled with her basket, so Dien stopped, shouldered the smaller girl's basket as well as her own, and then forged ahead. They reached the main square of the village just as a gathering was assembling in front of the village hall. They even had torches burning up the steps before the doors, so Dien guessed it had to be important. It looked like all the village had gathered.

"They're here," Helena said. She dumped her basket of squirmers, smoothed down her burgundy dress, and straightened her back. Dien plucked an errant squirmer from her friend's hair. She didn't much rate Helena's chances, not because her friend wasn't pretty enough, but because traders never married villagers. Still, it was good to have hope. That was something they all needed.

Dien placed her two baskets next to Helena's and joined her friend at the back of the crowd of villagers. Next to Helena in her burgundy, Dien looked too tall, too broad shouldered. All gangly and dreary. But that was fine; she wasn't looking to snatch a husband, but it might be she'd make Helena look better just standing near her. Luci stood on her other side, wringing her hands together and staring back into the forest.

"Can you see anything?" Helena asked.

The crowd of villagers was so thick there wasn't even space to squeeze in. Dien stood on her toes and peered over them. The Adjudicator, Menchen Ocha was sitting in his chair at the top of the steps. He could only walk for brief periods these days, so was mostly carried around in his chair when the village needed him. Behind the ancient man stood his wretched arse of a son, Donnel. There was another man stood beside Donnel who Dien didn't recognise. He was tall, pot-bellied, with no hair to speak of, and clothing far too fine to be from Berrywhistle.

"I think he's alone," Dien said.

"The trader?"

She nodded. "I can only see one. He's bald, Helena, and he has three chins."

Beside her, Helena sagged and kicked at a stone in the dirt.

"Chins are good," Luci said quietly.

They both looked at her and she went pale even in the dim light of the dying sun. "What? He must be successful if he can afford to eat." Dien chuckled at that and even Helena had to admit Luci had a point.

"Do you hear that?" Luci asked.

"Quiet now. Quiet!" Donnel Ocha shouted at the milling crowd. He grabbed a torch and waved it about in the air. Annoyingly, it had the desired effect and the villagers of Berrywhistle hushed to whispers.

Dien glanced about the crowd. She spotted her da by the one-room hut they called a tavern. He was leaning against the doorframe, his huge arms crossed over his chest, his brow furrowed in concentration. Dien decided to emulate him and turned her attention back to the Adjudicator.

Donnel opened his mouth to speak again, but his father interrupted him by slowly ambling out of his chair and climbed shakily to his feet. Despite his infirmity, the ancient Adjudicator had a powerful voice that demanded attention.

"Trader Samir has come from Rivern with dire news," the old man shouted. He nodded to the trader who took a hesitant step forward.

The villagers immediately started talking again, a wave of panicked voice rising like a flock of birds.

"Rivern is to the south, ain't it?"

"Dire means it's bad. Real bad."

"Quiet, you old fool. Let him talk."

The trader was shouting something, but Dien couldn't hear it over the clamour of the villagers. No one could.

"I have an awful feeling," Helena said. "In my gut."

Dien glanced to find her friend hugging herself. She put an arm around Helena's shoulders and pulled her close, found she was trembling.

"Hush!" Menchen Ocha bellowed, his powerful voice rolling over the crowd and silencing them like a wet blanket smothering a fire.

Far away, Dien heard a noise like a sharp whistle cut short.

The trader stepped forward again. For the first time, Dien noticed his clothes were dirty and dishevelled, as though he'd been wearing them for days, or even weeks. His chins were smudged with dirt and his eyes were wide and watery.

"Rivern has fallen," the trader shouted in a gravelly voice. "Demons came pouring out of the Southern Pass. More than we ever seen. They came straight for the village as if they knew it were there, not the swamps nor the mists protected us. They were led, they were, by a monster. Bigger than any demon I ever seen. He was riding a great demonic bear. The others bowed to him like a lord or something. Never seen anything like it."

The Adjudicator waved the trader back even as the villagers of Berrywhistle started shouting again, panic rising over them. Rivern gone. Black Crag gone. Dien thought maybe they were right to panic. The demons were flooding into their lands and none of the villages could stand against them.

Dien's da pushed away from the tavern door and stepped forward to the edge of the crowd. He was taller by a head than most of the other villagers and his voice carried over them. "Trader, are you saying..."

A scream ripped out from the forest, full of terror and pain. Everyone fell silent.

Dien turned to find Luci peering into the gloom of the trees, shaking. The little woman turned to Dien, eyes wide and full of fright. "I can hear them," she whispered.

"You fool!" Someone from the crowd shouted. "You led them right to us."

A man came charging out from the forest, staggering into trees as he ran. He was cradling his left arm against his chest. A brutal cut across his forehead had blood streaming down his face into his eyes. It was Panyet. Handsome Panyet injured and bleeding. He looked up, spotted the crowd of villagers, opened his mouth. A fleshy whip snapped out of the darkness, wrapped around his legs. Panyet fell forwards, smacked into the earthy ground hard. He groaned, looked up through sheeting blood, and dragged himself forward.

A clawed foot slammed down onto Panyet's back, pinning him to the soil. Dien looked up into the face of a demon leering at her.

The demon was tall, easily matching her da for height. It was rangy, with little horns poking out all along its arms and on its shaved scalp. Its skin was a motley of pinks and reds and blacks like it was badly burned. It wore hide britches and a tunic that looked like it was sewn from screaming human faces. In one taloned hand it carried a whip, the end still coiled around Panyet's legs. In its other it held a black metal sword with a serrated blade.

Two demonic hounds loped out of the darkness to either side of the monster. They were large as wolves. What fur they had was patchy and filthy, and spiky horns jutted from their skin around their shoulders. One of the hounds closed on Panyet, mouth opening. The demon hissed and the monster hound pulled back, cringing in fear.

The demon raised its chin and snuffed three times through a split nose. Then it gnashed pointed teeth together. The sound went through Dien, made her wince.

More demons stalked out of the darkness, stepping around trees and into the dim light of the Caped and Bone moons. Some were tall, some shorter, some brawny, and others painfully thin. They all had skin the colour of burns and bruises, swirling and mixing together, and horns erupting from their flesh. Some carried black metal weapons, swords and axes, others held nothing but whips or nets. All of them waited at the tree line, surrounding the village square. Surrounding the villagers.

The demon with the screaming face tunic stepped forward again, past the prone Panyet. It grinned, showing off pointed, bloody fangs, and raised its arms. Letting out a single whooping howl, it lowered its head and spoke.

"New meat!"

CHAPTER 2

Demon howls filled the air. The monsters sprang forward, closing in on the village square from every direction. The villagers of Berrywhistle broke, pushing, shoving, running. Blind panic devouring thought.

Someone smacked into Dien from behind, sent her sprawling. Her knees hit soil and a moment later she was up again, Helena's hands under her arm. Villagers were streaming all around them. Demons were hooting, snarling, snatching fleeing people as they ran, shoving them to the ground. Dien frantically searched for her da, but she couldn't see anything over the frenzy.

"We have to run," Helena shouted in her ear.

Dien grabbed Luci by the wrist, tugged both her friends into motion. She aimed for the tavern and ran. She had to find her da, he'd know what to do. He always knew what to do.

Another fleeing villager shoved into Dien. She didn't see who. She staggered away from the impact, kept on walking, all but dragging Helena and Luci with her. A gangly demon with weeping sores on its cheeks stalked towards them. Its eyes were fixed on her, black with malice, a greedy snarl on its lips. It reached for Dien, but Enna Rusk shoved past her and stumbled into the way of the demon. It snatched her instead and Enna let out a shriek as the monster threw her to the ground and fell atop her. Dien pressed on.

"Where are we going?" Helena shouted over the tumult. Dien didn't bother to answer. She didn't have an answer. She just needed to find her da.

By the time they shoved through the fleeing, panicking crowd and reached the tavern, her da was nowhere to be seen. Dien pulled both Helena and Luci to her. Luci immediately fell to her knees, buried her head in her hands. Helena was trembling, her burgundy dress torn around her legs, a cut on her cheek. People were crying, screaming, dying. Demons were whooping and howling, laughing. It was chaos.

The village hall was burning, flames already consuming the walls and licking greedily for the roof. Donnel and the trader were gone, but Menchen Ocha lay upon the steps. His chair had toppled and spilled the old Adjudicator out. He reached for it, pulled himself closer. The demon with the tunic of screaming faces started up the steps. He lashed his whip as he closed on the old man.

"Old meat. Weak meat." The demon thrust his jagged sword down into the Adjudicator's gut and ripped it out to the side, spraying blood across the steps. He turned and howled to the moons. Behind him, the village hall burned.

Dien grabbed Helena and Luci and ran. The forest swallowed them, trees on either side, darkness all around. Even the light of the two moons barely reached the forest floor. They barrelled on, Dien barely able to see past the tears in her eyes.

Something leapt out of the darkness, smashed into her. Dien fell, hit the ground hard, bashing her elbow. Hot blood washed down her arm but she ignored it, struggled back to her feet. Something snarled and she spun around to find one of the demon hounds stalking towards Helena.

Helena backed away, bumped into a tree. She was shaking. "Please don't. Please." She sank to her knees, sobbing.

Aren Tivers roared towards them, shouting and brandishing his oven paddle like an axe. He smacked the demon hound in the face, then spun the paddle around and stabbed the butt into its mouth.

"Get out of here. Go!" Aren shouted.

The demon hound bit down on the haft, snapped Aren's paddle in two, then leapt forward and ploughed into him, knocking him to the ground and savaging him with tooth and claw. Aren screamed in fear, in pain. The demon hound tore his chest to bloody ribbons with its claws, bit down on his arm, crunching bone.

Dien rushed past the slaughter and hauled Helena back to her feet. They had to run. To get away. Go anywhere that wasn't there. She looked around for Luci. The little woman was gone. Just gone. The hound was still tearing chunks out of Aren Tivers even though he had stopped screaming.

They ran on, stumbling through the dark, slipping around trees. Dien didn't know which direction they were headed anymore. Screams echoed through the forest, some cut short, others pleading, begging. Demons howled, growled, laughed. Some sounded so close Dien turned, certain the monsters had found them. But noise travelled strangely in the forest, especially at night, and there was nothing around them.

Time mushed into a confusing quagmire in her mind. Had it been minutes since the attack? Hours? She couldn't tell. It was a shock when they stumbled into the wooden wall of a cabin. One of the village homes with sturdy, insulated walls and planks of wood fitting together perfectly. Dien knew this hut, her father had built it. It belonged to the Tager sisters, Beryl and Marj. Dien's ma always joked they were older than the moons.

Helena sobbed, clasped a hand over her mouth. "They're dead," she whispered, her eyes wide and empty as a clean plate, her skin pale as milled flour. "They're all dead. Luci! Where's Luci? Where's Luci?" She sobbed again. "Mum, dad, please be alive. Please. Please. Please."

Dien grabbed her friend by the shoulders and shook her. Helena blinked a few times, tears rolling down her cheeks, and quieted.

"We'll look for them," Dien whispered. "I promise."

She edged around the cabin wall, still holding Helena's hand gone clammy in her grip. A scream echoed towards them but it sounded far off. The front door of the hut was open a jar, a hand lying on the doorstep keeping it open. There was a smear of blood on the wood. Dien turned away from it. Neither of them needed to look inside. At least she knew where she was now. She could find the way home.

The smell of smoke reached them. Far off, through the crowded trees and gloom of night, Dien saw the orange glows. Berrywhistle was burning. The demons were setting fire to everything. She realised then that they'd have nowhere to go. Even if they escaped, the village was done for. Gone. They'd have to flee.

"You might get your wish," Dien said quietly, already knowing it was a terrible thing to say but unable to stop herself. "We'll have to run to the Ice Plains. Eat fish. Learn to swim." She wiped a sleeve across her eyes. She felt so strange, so out of control.

Helena didn't answer. Just staggered along, feet sliding through fallen leaves, head darting about at every sound.

Another shrill scream echoed through the forest, followed by high-pitched pleading. Dien ignored it. She was almost home. Just a few more steps and she'd be able to see her cabin. Her ma and da would be there. They'd know what to do, where to go.

Dien heard raised voices, shouted accusations. She brushed past a large tree, still dragging Helena behind, and then her home was right there. There were four figures standing outside, three of them armed and facing off against one. Dien dropped Helena's hand and made to run to her da's aid, but a shape slipped from behind the nearest tree and grabbed her. A hand slid over her mouth, pulled her into the foliage. Dien bit the fingers across her mouth, tried to rise. She heard her ma's voice hiss in pain.

"Be still, Dien. Be still," her ma whispered in her ear. "Let your da handle this. Just hide here with me."

She craned her head. Her ma's face was drawn, streaked with dirt and tears, but her jaw was set and her eyes were hard. She kept one hand across Dien's mouth pulled Helena down into the bush with them. Dien tasted blood on her lips. Her ma's blood. She'd bitten her ma! She felt awful. People were dying, slaughtered by demons, the village was burning, and she'd just stumbled blind through the forest and bitten her own ma.

"You don't want to do this, Donnel," her da said loudly. He was standing in the doorway to their cabin, his hammer in both hands. Not any of his work hammers, but the other one. The big one. The one he never used but cleaned every day.

Donnel Ocha, Metwit Pa, and Iger Brane stood before him. Donnel and Metwit carried wood axes, Iger had a torch again. Dien couldn't understand it. Why were they here? Why were they accosting her da when there were demons killing everyone they knew?

"You brought them here, Unter Hostain, you did," Donnel snarled, waving his hatchet at her da.

Her da shook his head sadly. "The trader led them here, Donnel."

"It was you!" Donnel screamed, spittle flying from his mouth.

"The demons will hear," Helena whispered franticly. "They'll hear."

"Blood begets blood," Donnel continued. "And you are drowning in it, Unter Hostain. Peace Breaker. Demon Friend! We should ne'er have let you come here, no we should'na. I'll be fixing that mistake before we go, you mark me."

Her da was still as cold stone, his hammer in his hands. "You don't want to do this, Donnel," he repeated. "Please, I don't want to do this. Let's just go and save who we can."

"Save?" Donnel screeched. "SAVE? They're all dead because of you."

Donnel Ocha lurched forward, axe raised. Quick as a startled hare, her da shifted, slammed the butt of his hammer into the other man's face. Donnel dropped like a felled tree. Metwit and Iger closed on him all at once, from either side. Casual as breathing, Dien's da, swung his hammer out and to the side, sweeping Iger's feet from beneath him. Metwit chopped with his axe, but her da stepped aside as if he wasn't the biggest man in the village. Metwit stumbled, off balance. Her da slammed an elbow into his face and sent a knee into the smaller man's gut. Metwit teetered for a moment, then collapsed in a heap. It all happened in the space of two breaths, and her da had made it look so easy.

Iger's torch was on the floor, fire already catching on the nearby sticks and leaves, spreading. Dien had the urge to run for it again, like she had just that morning, pluck up the torch to keep their home from catching fire. But her ma's hand was tight across her mouth, holding her there.

Her da stared at the torch for a few seconds, watched the flames creep across the ground to the cabin, start licking at the wall. Then he turned away from it, as if he had just decided to let their home burn.

"I didn't want to do that, Donnel," her da said, his voice a rockslide. "I promise, I'll save everyone I can." Then he strode away from their burning home and the three men lying on the ground.

Donnel rolled over as her da passed him and flailed out. His hatchet bit deep into her da's ankle. He cried out, collapsed forward onto his knees, his foot almost severed by the blow.

Dien struggled, tried to rise, but her ma held her tight, surprisingly strong. She could hear a soft whining, felt her mother trembling, but still she held on, keeping Dien hidden in the bush.

Donnel rolled away, wrenching his hatchet free. Her da groaned, dropped his hammer and pressed a hand to his ankle, trying to stop the spurting blood. Metwit rose behind her da, his own axe flashing. He chopped it down into his back and Dien's da cried out again, arching.

They were felling him like a tree, one blow at a time. And Dien could do nothing. Nothing but watch. If she tried to help him they'd just cut her down too.

Donnel scrambled back to his feet, spitting leaves. The flames were climbing up the side of their hut now and the fire reflected in his bloody axe. Dien's da reached one shaking hand for his hammer, but Donnel stepped on it, pinning his fingers to the soil.

"Time to put an end to you for good an' all, Peace Breaker."

Donnel swung. Her da wrenched his hand back, making the smaller man stumble, then grabbed his hammer. Too late. Donnel's hatchet thudded into her da's neck.

"Die in shame, Unter Hostain," Donnel said. Then he spat in her da's face and wrenched his hatchet free.

Blood sluiced down her da's neck, soaking his shirt. So much blood.

Somewhere close by, a demon howled.

"Burn it," Donnel said as he stalked off towards the forest. Metwit ran after him. Iger Brane snatched up the torch, tossed the brand inside their cabin, then followed.

Dien slumped, sobbed into her mother's hand still pressed firmly over her mouth. Her da was dead. It wasn't right. Couldn't be true. He was too strong to die. But there he was, bloody and slumped over. Gone. All his skill, kindness, knowledge, and love were gone. The world had lost something too good for it. Dien had lost the most important thing in her life. She doubled over, sobbed again, whined, realised she was screaming into her ma's hand.

"Hush now. Hush!" Her ma's voice was harsh in her ear.

Dien didn't want to be quiet. Her blood was fire in her veins as surely as the flames eating away at her home. She wanted to scream, to rage, to chase down Donnel and tear him apart. But she clamped her mouth shut, wiped a dirty sleeve across her eyes. Beside her, Helena was trembling, eyes open so wide it looked painful. Dien had seen the like before after wild bear attacks. Some folk went into shock and just stopped being for a time.

One of the demon hounds padded into the clearing. It snuffed the air, then loped forward to Dien's da. She wanted to run at it, throw rocks at it, scare it away. But how could she hope to scare a demon? The hound took a big sniff, then pawed at her da. He slumped over sideways, hit the ground. The demon leapt on him.

Dien's ma pulled her and Helena away, through the bushes as quietly as possible. The noise of the demon savaging her da's body made her sick.

The whoops of demons continued to echo through the trees. There were no more screams though, only the occasional sobbing. Had to be villagers, Dien couldn't imagine a demon crying. They were too monstrous, too evil.

They crept through the forest. Helena walked where she was pulled like a child's toy on a rope. But Dien's ma was a rock, leading them with a strength she had never seen in the woman before.

A stick snapped somewhere close. Dien's ma dragged both of them down and pressed them back against a tree. There were no bushes to hide in, so all they could do was cling to the shadows.

"Find more. More meat. Go soon," barked a guttural voice. Talons scraped at the bark on the other side of the tree, then gone as the demon stalked away into the forest.

Her ma' pulled them back to their feet, stared into Dien's eyes. "If we get separated, go to the kiln caves. They'll never find you in there."

Dien trembled, wanted to say something, but didn't know what. Instead, she just nodded.

"Good girl," her ma said and pulled her into a brief hug, squeezed her tight. "Now move."

They ran as quickly as possible, keeping to the soft leaves where they could hide their footfalls. It was only a short walk to the caves, shorter at a run.

A stone whipped out of the darkness, smacked into her ma and sent her sprawling with a cry of pain. Dien grabbed hold of Helena, hugged her tight and pulled her to a stop.

Her ma looked up at Dien, face pained, arm hanging awkwardly. "Go!"

"Got one. Running meat," this demon's voice was reedy. It stalked out of the darkness, small but swarthy, skin bleeding around its horns. It looked up at Dien and Helena. "More meat. Good catch."

"Run!" her ma shrieked.

Dien clutched Helena, dragged her about, turned to run. Another demon stepped from the darkness in front of them. Dien recognised it, the screaming faces on its jerkin marking it out from the others. It stared down at them, gnashed its teeth once.

"Caught meat," said the smaller demon. "Good catch." It grabbed Dein's ma around the thigh and pulled her closer. Her ma kicked at it with her other leg and caught the demon in the chin. The demon laughed, raked talons along her ma's leg. Her ma screamed as claws ripped her flesh.

The lead demon hissed and stalked closer to the smaller one. "Wounded meat. Weak meat. Not walking."

The smaller demon whined, cowered, held up its hands.

Dien caught her mother's eyes. Saw her mouth *Go!* She grabbed Helena's hand, turned, and ran.

The demon's whip snapped out, wrapped around Dien's legs. She pitched forward, hit the ground hard, her head bouncing off a knot of roots and making her vision swim. Helena slowed to a stop, stood there, staring wide eyed at nothing. Not running. Not getting away.

"Earta, come. Eira, come." The lead demon bellowed.

Dien rolled over, groaning. Her head hurt like an insect was trying to claw its way inside her skull. She blinked away the fuzzy edges. Her ma was crawling through the dirt towards her, tears streaming down her face.

The two demon hounds loped out of the darkness, their muzzles wet and dripping blood. The lead demon sniffed once, then pointed at Dien's ma. "Eat meat."

The hounds pounced on her ma, biting, savaging, clawing. She screamed and Dien screamed with her.

CHAPTER 3

The first few days passed in a blur. They walked, tied together with rough ropes woven from hair that rubbed the skin of Dien's wrists raw. She knew that should hurt, yet it didn't. The demons beat them awake and whipped them into motion each morning, and the villagers marched, first through forest, then onto grassy hills. She knew her feet should hurt, her legs should ache. Yet they didn't. Even the lashing whips the demons dealt out barely reached her. She was just numb.

Dien had never left the forest before. She'd been to the edge twice, both to Wraith Lake, which barely counted as a lake and had no wraiths that she had ever seen, and to Hookstone where she had stared out into the fields and wondered just how big the world truly was. During the summer, the grass was a brilliant emerald that shone in sunlight, waved in the wind, a stunning contrast to the azure sky above. In winter, soft snow blanketed the land as far she could see. She and Helena and Luci had played in the white powder, gathering it up and throwing it at each other. They had been much younger then. Dien had been thoroughly chastised by her parents for venturing so far. What if there had been demons outside the forest? What if the three girls had been seen?

It all seemed so pointless now. Despite all those years hiding, despite the caution, the demons had come. Berrywhistle was gone, half the village slaughtered. Her parents were dead. That should hurt. Dien knew that should hurt deep inside, like an icy claw digging nails into her heart. Yet it didn't. She felt nothing.

Others were hurting. Some of the villagers cried occasionally, some cried all the time, and all did it quietly. The demons didn't like it when they wailed, and the brutal beatings had convinced them all to silence, or as near to it as they could manage. Beryl Tager had been too noisy on the first day. She had cried and cried, mourning the death of her twin. Even when the demons beat her, she had wept. Then the demon with the screaming face jerkin had arrived. He cut Beryl free from the train of trussed up villagers and dragged her away. No one had seen Beryl Tager since. They all knew what that meant. Dien thought that, too, should hurt. She had known Beryl Tager all her life, had been placed in her care for a half sun now and then when she was younger. The old spinster had always smelled of honey and hummed to herself. She had been kind. She was gone now, as dead as her twin sister, Marj. Still Dien didn't feel anything. But she knew she should. She wanted to feel again.

Helena had survived. She was tied to Dien, behind her in the train. Her once lovely burgundy dress was ruined; ripped and torn, stained with mud and blood. She marched along in weary sorrow. Occasionally she'd sob, her grief swelling up and consuming her — her parents were not in the train and that meant they, too, were dead, but Helena was smart enough to stifle her tears before the demons took notice. Sometimes, she spoke, offering words of encouragement like *'At least we're still alive.'* Dien wasn't sure if her friend meant the words for her or for herself. She wanted to offer some in return, but nothing came to mind, so she trudged on, silent and sullen. Numb.

Luci had also survived. She was tied to the train of villagers far behind so Dien saw little of her during the days when they marched. On the third night after the slaughter, when they huddled together in small circles, she caught a real glimpse of her friend. Luci had taken a beating and her face was swollen in a motley of bruises. One eye was puffy and red from tears, the other one sealed closed with a weeping scab. She rubbed at her fingers constantly, as if trying to clean them without water. Dien met the woman's eye once and Luci had tried a cracked-lipped smile at her. She was missing a tooth and her gums were bloody. Dien quickly looked away, but not swiftly enough. Her friend's suffering reached her. Sadness and sorrow and the desire, the deep need to go to her and comfort her.

That swell of emotion unlocked something inside. Seeing her friend in so much pain and still forcing out a smile lifted the latch, and the doorway to Dien's own heart swung open. And inside was nothing but pain and grief.

Her parents were dead. Murdered. It was impossible. Her da had always been there, a giant of a man, gentle power, and indomitable good will. Gone. Her ma, so quiet and small, but fierce in her love of her family and her community. Gone. Both of them gone. And so many more besides. Menchen Ocha, gone. Aren Tivers, the Tager sisters, Rankin and Lola Tressel, Yona and Enrit Yolk. Gone, gone, gone. All gone!

Dien squeezed her eyes shut, felt tears cascading down her cheeks. She forced her arm into her mouth, filthy sleeve and all, clenched her teeth around her own flesh and screamed out her grief.

Someone shook her and she opened her eyes. Helena was beside her, an arm on her knee, shaking her insistently.

"Quiet!" her friend hissed, then lowered eyes to stare at the ground. Everyone lowered their gaze as though the patchy grass and pitted earth between them was the most interesting thing any of them had ever seen.

Dien looked up. The demons were approaching like they did every night, each one carrying little wooden bowls they had stolen from the village as they sacked it. Feeding time. Every day some of the demons ventured out, hunting, came back with deer or rabbits or anything else they could catch. The villagers were fed just enough to keep them all alive. To keep them marching... wherever they were going.

Now Dien thought about it, she had no idea where they were being led. The demons were moving them west and south, away from the forest, towards the giant mountains with their peaks forever white. South, where the demons heralded from.

A demon swaggered towards their group of ten, all huddled together. It had pinkish skin swathed with patchy red like oil dashed against cloth. It had only one horn on its head and a few scattered down its arms. Dien wondered if so few horns meant it was a young demon. It had almost human feet, but with thick skin and long, sharp nails. No shoes. None of the demons wore shoes of any kind. Some didn't wear clothes at all, and others wore tattered rags as if to mock the humans they drove.

Dien stared at the demon, studying it. When it noticed, it snarled, cracked lips pulling back to reveal pointed teeth. It dropped one of the bowls it was carrying at Dien's feet and struck. The back of its taloned hand cracked against her cheek and she was flung to the earth, mewling in pain. The demon was a skinny thing but its blow was so much harder than Metwit's had been. Her face felt like it had been rent in two there was such pain.

"No look. Weak meat. Eyes down," the demon stalked away.

Helena helped Dien sit upright as other demons brought more bowls to the rest of the villagers. They all accepted the food without looking up. Dien rescued her own bowl and scooped as much spilled broth into it as she could. It was mostly dirt by the time she was done. Helena poured some of her own watery broth out into Dien's bowl. It wasn't much, but such a simple act of kindness made Dien ache inside.

The broth was weak, a trace of meaty flavour but little else. They all slurped it down in silence and then lay out to sleep upon the cold earth. All of them knew it would not be long until they were hauled up to start marching all over again.

Dien lay there, shivering in her threadbare dress, and thought about her parents. They were dead. And she, and all the survivors of Berrywhistle, were now demon thralls. She had no idea what happened to those who were captured by demons. There were always stories of the raids, of those taken. There were never stories of anyone escaping.

The next day Dien felt renewed. She could feel again, though mostly she felt pain. Her face stung and ached in equal measure where the demon had struck her. Her mouth was swollen and her lips throbbed, but that only distracted her from the pain in her legs and feet. She had never walked so far in a day before, let alone four days of marching at a gruelling pace set by demons with inhuman strength who never tired. Her feet had knives driving up through her soles and into her heels. But still she walked. She had no choice. None of them did.

The demons led them to a stream, waited while the villagers drank, then pushed them on. They stalked along beside the train of captured villagers, keeping their distance, but also penning them in on both sides. There was no chance of escape, especially not while they were tied to each other. The demons travelled in small groups, barking laughter between each other, trading harsh words in some language Dien couldn't understand. She listened, straining her ears to hear them, but it all sounded like guttural growls and crooning rasps to her ear. Occasionally, one of the demons would stalk closer and whip one of the villagers and shout, "Walking meat. Faster walk. Keep walk."

The demon hounds were even worse. They ranged ahead or behind, often disappearing with the hunters and returning with red muzzles. Dien hated the hounds. She remembered the noise of them tearing into her da's body, the sight of them ripping her ma apart even as she screamed for mercy. Useless screams. There was no mercy in demons. There was nothing good in them at all.

Her da had once told Dien there was good in everyone, even those who do bad things. Dien scoffed at that now. What did he know? Her da had been murdered by Donnel and his friends even as the demons ravaged the village. He had been kind and honourable, and where had it gotten him? Dien wanted to hate him for that. If he had just fought back properly, made sure Donnel Ocha couldn't get back up. If he had just been a little less kind… But she couldn't hate him. If he had been less kind, he wouldn't have been the da she loved so.

Donnel Ocha had survived, along with Metwit and Iger Brane. They walked behind Dien, part of Luci's train of thralls. She stared at them from time to time, hated them for all they had done. Her da wouldn't like that, she knew, but they had murdered him and they deserved her hatred.

It was mid-sun on the fourth day when the first villager collapsed. The hunters hadn't brought back any food the day before, and humans and demons both had gone hungry.

Up ahead, someone cried out. The train of marching villagers slowed. Dien leaned to the side to see what was happening. She wasn't the only one. The demons closed in like snarling wolves. Dien caught a whip to her back, the snapping end striking between her shoulder blades. She felt fresh blood dribbling down her skin and quickly shuffled back into line. Helena inched forwards, tugging on her own ropes to drag the others faster for a few seconds. She patted at Dien uselessly as though a few gentle touches could somehow heal the new wound.

The line trailed to a stop as the villagers waited behind the commotion. Dien risked stepping to the side again to peer forwards. Someone had fallen and was not getting up. A whisper trailed back through the line of villagers. It was Old Swiff. Everyone knew he had a bad knee, an injury that had never healed quite right. Old Swiff liked to say he'd got it fighting wolves, but Dien's da had told her the truth once. Old Swiff had taking a bad step into a ditch when drunk on moonshine one night. He'd twisted his knee so bad it had popped right out of the socket. It had taken three men to hold him still while Arnut Poll wrenched it back into place.

The lead demon with the screaming tunic stalked past Dien. She shuffled back into line quickly. The demon shoved others out of the way, then reached down and hauled Old Swiff back to his feet as easily as Dien's da had picked her up when she was a child.

"Up, meat. Walking meat. No stop," the demon snarled.

"I can't," Old Swiff cried. Dien heard him even twenty paces away with the other villagers whispering between them. "My knee, it's..."

The demon struck him back to the muddy ground. "No talking. Walking meat."

The demon bent down. Old Swiff screamed, gagged, gurgled. The train of villagers started milling, shuffling, panicking. When the demon stood again, it had a scrap of bloody flesh in its taloned hand. Dien realised in horror it was Old Swiff's tongue. The monster had ripped it straight out of his mouth.

"Sun and Moons!" Helena swore from behind and gagged. The villagers cursed, shambling. Miss Trudie screamed but only briefly as Arnut Poll stepped in close and clasped a dirty hand around her mouth.

Dien clutched Helena even as her friend fell to her knees. She dragged her upright. "Don't," she whispered urgently.

"That was his tongue. Sun and Moons, Dien. His tongue."

"Quiet!" Dien hissed. She couldn't let Helena be taken next.

The demon waved the severed tongue about for a few more moments, then tossed it to the dirt. Old Swiff was still making gagging noises. Dien was glad she couldn't see him. Then the demon stalked back through the train of villagers and grabbed Old Swiff, cutting his bonds and dragging him out of the line. The demon threw him to the ground next to his tongue. He was gushing blood, choking on it, clutching at his face.

"Earta, come. Eira, come." The demon shouted.

Dien heard a low growl from behind and startled as the two demon hounds stalked past her and Helena, one on each side. She got a good look at their rangy, discoloured fur. One of the beasts had sabrefangs jutting from its jaw, the other did not. She wondered if that made them different breeds. The hounds closed on the lead demon, stalking low to the ground.

The demon pointed at Old Swiff and gnashed his teeth. "Eat meat."

It was just like before. Just like her ma. The demon hounds pounced on Old Swiff and tore into him, tooth and claw. He screamed, gurgled. Then he stopped and somehow that was worse. Helena turned away, buried her head in Dien's shoulder. But Dien did not turn away. She watched it all in mute horror as the demons disembowelled Old Swiff.

After the hounds were done, their bellies full, the lead demon tore away the last of Old Swiff's trailing innards then picked up his corpse as if it weighed no less than a twig. The demon carried the corpse over to the four-wheel cart and draped it over the side of the wooden railing. It was Panyet and Donnel's turn to pull the cart today and both of the young men recoiled at the corpse, but a hiss from the demon soon got them back behind the bar to pull it along.

The cart bounced as Panyet and Donnel started hauling it onwards, and the blanket covering it shifted. Dien caught a glimpse of a hunk of square metal in the back. She recognised it. Solid metal, perfectly forged, a haft of ironwood running through it, boar-hair rope tied around the haft. Her da's hammer. The demons must have taken it from his body.

"Walking meat!" the lead demon bellowed and within moments the train of villagers had been whipped back into motion. They trudged along in silence, no one willing to be the next to fall. Old Swiff's bleeding corpse was too fresh a reminder.

The light was failing by the time the demons stalked down the line shouting at them all to stop. They huddled into groups of ten, all of them tied to others with the hairy ropes around their wrists. Dien's skin itched at the irritation, but there was nothing she could do about it. They were in a grassy field, thick with thistles and biting bugs. Dien sank onto her knees and groaned. Her legs somehow ached even more now that she wasn't walking. She wasn't alone in her misery, but that just made it worse.

The demons paid them little attention but to saunter past occasionally, checking on them all. Then they started fires, four of them, each one sparking, roaring, smoking. A beacon in the night. Dien stared at the flames in wonder. She'd never seen fires so large. Back at the village, the oven fires were kept low and smouldering, the kilns were hidden deep underground, and the occasional torches they lit were tiny flames. She was fascinated. She wanted to get up and walk over to it, to warm her hands on the blaze.

The demons gathered around the fires, talking in their harsh tongue. Some laughed. One of the monsters with big bug eyes kept glancing at

Dien's group of huddled villagers, licking its lips. She looked away quickly whenever that demon looked her way. But she soon started watching them again. Studying them, measuring them just as her da' had said.

Big metal pots were hung over the fires, filled from a nearby stream with icy water and then left to boil. In the light of the fires, Dien saw a couple of demons strolling between the pots. They kept adding things to the water, stirring them with sticks, then moving on.

A whisper started among the villagers, passing through first one group and then onto another. Dien strained her ears, waited impatiently for the whispers to reach her group.

"Quiet, meat!" roared a demon as it stalked by. It was dragging something along the ground, towards the closest of the fires.

"Sun and Moons, no," whispered Enna Rusk through swollen lips.

Dien half rose, just enough to see, then quickly flopped back down. She wished she hadn't looked.

"What is it?" Helena asked. "Dien?"

Dien shook her head. She tried to form the words. Couldn't.

"It's Swiff," Enna Rusk spat. "They're cuttin' him up."

"Why?" Helena asked.

"Quiet, meat!" another demon roared. They all fell silent. It didn't matter. They all knew what the demons were doing. They could see it plain as day as a pot-bellied demon with black and brown skin worked at Old Swiff's corpse with a cleaver, cracked his bones, chopped his flesh into strings of bloody meat. Other demons grabbed bits of Old Swiff, tossed them into the pots, stirred the contents. They were stripping his meat from his bones, cooking him, making a stew from the kind old man who spoke about his chickens like they were children.

Dien was still watching hours later when the demons started to eat. They gathered around the two fires furthest from the huddled villagers, ladled meaty, bloody broth into bowls and slurped it down. One of the demons, a younger one judging by the fewer horns, tried to go back to the pot for a second helping. One of the older demons knocked the younger one down with a strike that should have broken bones. All the demons jeered, the younger one included.

Then came feeding time. Dien watched in horror as the demons scooped broth from the pots hanging over the two closer fires. She could only guess the monsters had put the scraps and bones in those pots. Each of the villagers was given a bowl and they all knew now what they would be eating.

Dien stared down at the bowl in her lap, felt bile stinging her throat.

"No waste," shouted one of the demons. "Eat now." It laughed and walked away.

They all stared down at the bowls. Each of them knew it was the only food they would get. And yet, they knew what it was. They had all known Old Swiff, had lived with him for years, named him friend. But they were starving, already existing on meagre portions, and forced to walk all day.

The bald trader was the first to lift the bowl to his lips. Dien stared at him aghast as he slurped the broth. Then she heard someone else eating. It was Enna Rusk. The older woman met Dien's gaze as she chewed, swallowed. She looked disgusted but she didn't stop. One by one, villagers started eating the broth. Eating Old Swiff. It was awful. It was disgusting. But Dien found she couldn't blame them. They were just doing what they had to to survive. They all had to do whatever they needed to survive now. That was all that was left to them.

Dien stared down at the bowl filled with congealing brown broth. There was a chunk of something floating in it. *Something*. She refused to think about what that something was.

"Dien?" Helena said in a voice so quiet she barely heard it over the slurping of the other villagers. "What do we do?"

Dien poked at the bowl. The contents wobbled and the chunk dipped below the surface and then back up again. She tipped it further and further until the broth started to spill over the side.

The bald trader shoved into Dien with his elbow, knocked her over. He grabbed the bowl before it spilled. "Stupid girl!" the man hissed at her. Then he raised the bowl to his lips and started eating.

Beside Helena, the young woodsmen with a twitchy eye, grabbed her untouched bowl. Helena didn't try to stop him. Almost half the villagers ate the broth that night, even knowing where it came from. The rest of them starved.

Dien lay on her side for a few moments, feeling the soft, cold earth beneath her. This was her life now. She realised with a desperate pang that there was no going back. This was why the demons called them all meat. Because that's what they were. Nothing but meat as surely as the chickens Old Swiff had raised. They were all just waiting their turn to be next in the pots.

Except, that couldn't be all it was. They were going somewhere. The demons were driving them steadily towards the mountains. Dien doubted whatever was waiting for them there would be any better. They had to escape, to find a way free. Somehow.

She dug her fingers into the dirt, squeezing a handful in her fist just to feel like she had power over something. A worm wriggled between her fingers. A little squirmer. Desperate to escape her grip. To survive.

Dien remembered the first time her da had taken her hunting. It had been winter, snow so heavy it packed the trees above and fell through to coat the forest floor as well. Each footstep had crunched and every breath misted into the dingy morning light.

They'd come across a bear, its back leg all torn and bloody. The beast was leaning against a tree that had been scraped almost clean of bark by raking claws. A thin coat of snow had fallen over the beast lining its fur.

Dien had taken it for dead. At just ten winters old, she'd never seen a bear before, dead or otherwise. She'd tried to approach, but her da pulled her back, made her crouch in a bush. They watched the bear for almost an eighth of a sun, until Dien was trembling from the cold. Still it didn't move, not so much as a breath stirring its lungs.

"It's dead," Dien said, blowing warm air into her hands.

"Is it?" her da asked. He waved her back, behind a tree and out of sight. Then he stood, rustling the bush as he did.

The bear cracked open a single eye, sighted her da, then lurched unsteadily to its feet. It let out a pained roar that turned to a wheeze and then great rattling breaths. But it faced her da, held its ground. Even wounded as it was.

Dien's da held up his hands and backed slowly into the bush. He took Dien by the hand and dragged her away, keeping his eye on the wounded bear all the while.

"I don't understand," Dien said once they were out of sight. "It's dying. In pain. Why did it try to fight you? What was the point of scaring you away?"

Her da smiled down at her and folded his arms. "Survival, little bug. That's always the point. The only reason for anything. Even when all is lost and you're too wounded to go on, the bear fights to survive. Because that's all it has. All it ever had. Life. Its own life. It won't give up, not ever. Not while it has even a chance of survival." He bent down in front of her. Even squatting on his haunches, he'd been taller than her. "And that, little bug, is why you never go near a bear. Even when you think it's dead."

Dien sat up, holding the worm between her fingers. She stared at it for a moment, then bit it in half and swallowed before she could taste it or feel it wriggling in her mouth. The other half continued to squirm. She held it out to Helena.

"We survive," Dien said. "That's what we do, Helena. We survive."

CHAPTER 4

The march continued, day after day, ever onwards towards mountains that never seemed to get any closer. Dien's sandals fell apart, the straps fraying and then snapping, and yet on she walked. She felt every stone, sliced her feet to bloody ribbons, had to pick dirt and thorns from her skin. But she couldn't stop. She carried the worn out remains of her sandals and that night wove new straps from grass fronds.

It was three days after Old Swiff when the hunters returned with no food and the demons picked their next victim. No one had fallen, no one had stopped. So when they made camp for the night and got the fires going, the lead demon with his screaming face jerkin stalked among them, gnashing his teeth and hauling villagers to their feet to check them over. No one wanted to be noticed, so everyone kept their heads down. Even Dien, though it shamed her to do it. She prayed to the Moons and Sun that the demon wouldn't pick her, wouldn't pick Helena or Luci. But it felt like a betrayal. Wishing it wouldn't be one of them was only hoping it would be someone else.

The demon took one look at Iger Brane's clubhand and slashed through his bonds, hauling him out and throwing him to the ground. Iger cried, pleaded, screamed.

Then came the words. "Earta come. Eira come. Eat meat." And the demon hounds ripped Iger apart, tearing out his guts and feasting on his entrails. Dien watched, caught between horror and satisfaction. Iger had been one of the three who had murdered her da. Now he was dead. She was glad. She was sick. She was terrified.

When the bowls of Iger stew were dropped in their laps, most of the villagers paused again. Almost half of them had eaten Old Swiff in the end, but that was one time and now they realised it would happen again and again. Now they were starting to wonder how many of their friends they would have to eat before they reached their destination. Dien wondered if any of them really thought things would change once the demons had driven them to the mountains. In the end, Donnel Ocha was the first to tuck in and slurp a bowlful of his former friend. Others quickly followed. More of them giving in to their growling stomachs until only eight villagers refused to eat.

Dien didn't eat. She just sat with her bowl of person congealing in front of her until one of the other villagers, someone she had called a friend, reached out and took her serving. She didn't even bother looking at who it was. It didn't matter. They were doing what they needed to survive, and so was she.

The next day it rained. A relentless icy downpour turned the ground to sucking mud that squelched through Dien's toes and made each step a heroic effort. The going was tougher, but the demons drove them on at the same pace, whipping anyone who slowed. Twice Helena fell and Dien tugged on the hairy rope to pull her friend back up before the demons could take notice. After the second time, Dien held Helena close and they struggled on together. It was a painful, miserable day made worse by the lack of food. Both of them refused to eat the villager stew. They plucked bugs from the grass or mud wherever they could, chewed on reeds until they were soft enough to swallow. It wasn't much. It wasn't enough. Yet they marched on.

Dien stopped counting days. There seemed little point. Time was marked by the demons growing hungry enough to stalk through the captured villagers and pick one of them to kill and eat. At first, Dien thought they were choosing those who looked weakest or oldest, those unlikely to survive the journey. But then the lead demon picked Rory Keener, a bull of a man who had been chosen to pull the cart five times already. Dien barely knew Rory except that her da had enjoyed drinking and gaming with him at the tavern. Rory tried to fight back, threw a punch at the demon. It didn't even stagger from the blow, just laughed and felled the big man with a single strike. There was no hesitation in most of the villagers by the time Rory was butchered. Only three of them were still refusing to eat and Dien had the suspicion Helena would have given in if not for her own stubborn resistance.

The days dragged on. Dien felt herself growing lean, then skinny as the flesh fell from her. Her feet grew callouses, stopped hurting, no longer bled from every stone she trod on. Her old pale dress was little more than greying rags, itchy and alive with lice. Her dark hair was matted with filth and her skin was greasy. And on they marched, towards the mountains. She couldn't quite understand how they hadn't reached them yet. She started to wonder if they ever would, or if this was life now, one dragging step after another, slowly picked out of the crowd and eaten, an endless march to nowhere with the only release being death.

They were down to twenty-two villagers, from the original thirty who had been captured, when Dien finally saw something change. The demons started growing agitated as they marched through the first season's first snowflakes. She had learned to watch them, listen to when they sounded angry or hungry. But the time was wrong. Only yesterday, they had killed miss Trudie, thrown her into the pots. Never again would anyone sit at her feet and learn the old rhymes telling them which plants they could eat and which they could not.

More demons walked into view, a second band driving captured humans of their own. Another village maybe, gone now. Dien peered at them eagerly, hoping they had not yet given up like her own people. But she could tell by the way they slogged on, heads hung in weary resignation that it was a vain hope.

This new group was larger; more captured villagers, more demons. The demon with the screaming tunic approached the other group and was met by a brutish demon with a rounded belly and arms as thick as Dien's waist. He had over a dozen little horns sticking from his scalp. They stopped a wary distance from each other, snapped words back and forth. The brute pointed towards the mountains. Screaming Tunic growled, took a step forward. The brute thumped his chest with a taloned hand and grinned, showing off sharp teeth. The two demons were of a height, but the brute was so brawny he seemed to tower over the other.

Screaming Tunic roared and threw himself at the brute. The brute staggered back a step then bellowed and met Screaming Tunic claw to claw, pushing the smaller demon down.

Demons from both groups whooped and flocked to watch, leaving the villagers unguarded for the first time since their capture so many days ago. Dien stared at the gathering, her view of the fight obscured by so many bodies. Then she dropped down, into the swaying grass and started searching the ground.

"What are you doing?" Helena asked, crouching next to her.

"I need a stone," Dien said, patting at the ground.

The bald trader, Samir, stared down at her aghast. "Don't do anything stupid, girl." Dien ignored him and kept searching.

A cheer went up from the gathered demons, followed by braying laughter. Dien heard frustrated growling and hoped it meant the fight was still ongoing. She found a stone with a sharp enough edge she cut her thumb on it and started sawing at the rope that bound her to the trader.

"You're mad, girl," the trader hissed. "They'll put you in the pot."

"What do you care?" Dien shot back, still sawing at the rope.

"There's nothing on you. You won't feed us all."

Dien stopped for a moment, stared up at the man. He really didn't care about her. He only cared that he might go hungry, that he might not have someone to eat for a few days. It was horrifying that people—her people—had been so changed in so short a time. She looked at the other villagers, folk she had known all her life. Some were watching the fight, others were just staring down at her, eyes gazing at her stick thin arms.

No doubt thinking the same as the trader, that she was too skinny to give them a real meal.

Her da had said you did whatever you needed to survive, but was it really surviving if you lost who you were along the way? She shook her head, grit her teeth, and went back to sawing at the rope. They might lose themselves, but she would not.

Helena's hands closed over Dien's, gripped them feebly. Her fingers were as thin and bony as Dien's. They were both starving. Helena shook her head. "Stop, Dien."

"We have to escape. Run. I can't... I can't be here. Helena, now is our chance to escape."

"Where?" Helena said. She took a hand away, waved it around. "Look, Dien. There's nothing but grass and earth for days. If you run, they'll catch you." She met Dien's stare and there were tears in her eyes. "Please don't leave me alone."

Dien hung her head and sighed. She dropped the stone. A mighty cheer went up from the gathered demons. Dien stood slowly, suddenly exhausted. Helena helped her stand, steadied her when she swayed on her feet.

"We will escape," Dien whispered. "Both of us."

"I know," Helena said.

"I promise!"

Helena nodded. "But not now."

In the middle of the crowd of demons, Screaming Tunic stood, holding the brute's severed head above him in two claws. Blood ran from the head and Screaming Tunic opened his mouth and let it drip down his throat. He tossed the head aside, spread his arms wide and screamed at the blue sky.

Dien leaned against Helena and watched as the demons cavorted, whooped, hollered. At some point she realised they were all chanting something, a single word over and over. "Swordere. Swordere. Swordere." And suddenly she realised she had heard it before, many times. It was a name. It was Screaming Tunic's name. The realisation staggered Dien, though she wasn't sure why. The demons had names.

There was no more marching that day. The two bands of demons merged, camping together. Fires were lit, pots were filled from a nearby river. There was a festive mood in the air. It reminded Dien of the turning of seasons, when winter gave way to spring and the days started to lengthen once again.

Berrywhistle had always made a celebration of those times. As far back as Dien could remember, it had been a time of joy. Great feasts were laid out with everyone in the village gathering together, eating, drinking, dancing, singing. Telling stories. Dien had always loved the Springtide festival. Her da let her drink from his beer while ma wasn't watching. Dien hated the taste, but that was never the point. It was a little secret she and her da shared, something that was theirs and no one else's. And it gave Dien a fuzzy head which only made the stories more engrossing. She wasn't much of a dancer, couldn't hold a note to sing, but she loved to hear the tall tales some of the elders wove.

No one made a story come alive quite like Menchen Ocha. The Adjudicator had a commanding voice and a talent for drama. Even after his back failed him, restricting him to his chair, and his voice took on the phlegmy croak of laboured breathing, everyone vied for a place to sit before his chair and listen to him. Dien particularly loved Swallowtail.

Swallowtail was a story about a young girl who lived in a forest. She was born with a malformed leg that made her forever in pain, limping and unable to run like the other children. But one thing Swallowtail could always do was climb and she was forever scaling trees to stare at the sky. She watched the birds soaring in the endless blue and envied them their freedom, for the birds were masters of a realm that no human could ever touch.

Swallowtail tried building herself wings from sticks and feathers plucked from chickens. She limped along the forest floor as fast as she could, flapping and flapping while her fellow villagers mocked her. But no matter how hard she flapped, or how high she jumped, she could never get off the ground. She climbed a small tree and leapt from it, only to come crashing to the ground. Her makeshift wings snapped back to the kindling they were and Swallowtail fled from the laughter of the others.

For hours the young girl limped through the forest, weeping for her broken dream of joining the birds in the sky. Then she heard a shrill tweeting and followed the sound to a small starling hopping furiously on the forest floor. One of its wings was bent and broken, and it couldn't fly.

Swallowtail gathered the little starling into her arms and limped back to her village. She showed the bird to her mother who only shook her head and said there was nothing to be done for the creature. A broken wing could no more heal than Swallowtail's malformed leg. Better to put the beast out of its misery. There was little meat on a creature so small, but perhaps enough for a single meal and so its strength would become theirs.

Swallowtail clutched the bird to her chest and fled her mother, crying as loudly as the starling in her arms. She came across the tallest tree in the forest, the only one she'd never before had the courage to climb. Holding the starling tight, Swallowtail scaled the tree with a skill no one else could match, not even those with two working legs. When she came to the top of the tree, she stared up at the sky and held the starling aloft, wishing for it to flap its wings and take flight. The bird twitched in her arms, then let out a mournful whistle. It was as broken as she was.

Remembering her mother's words about the starling's strength becoming their own, Swallowtail shoved the bird in her mouth and swallowed. Then she spread her arms wide and leapt from the tallest tree in the forest. Girl and bird became one in a glorious transformation and Swallowtail grew wings that carried her into the sky. Apart they had both been broken, but together, girl and bird were masters of earth and sky.

It was a foolish tale, Dien knew, but she had always liked it. She wished she could grow wings now, to fly away and escape the demons. But wishing for things had no greater effect than praying to the Moons and Sun. If she truly wanted to escape, she would have to do as Swallowtail and make it happen herself. She just needed to bide her time, watch the demons, measure them.

The two groups of villagers were brought together. The new group was easily twice as large as the survivors from Berrywhistle, but they were just as broken. They moved slowly, eyes downcast. Even once all the humans were picketed together, and most of the demons were celebrating around the fires, the newcomers didn't talk except to answer brief questions. They were from a small mountain range to the north, a village called Sireridge. There had been more of them, many more, but now there weren't.

From out of the large cart the other group had been dragging, the demons pulled furs; great armfuls of them. They dumped the furs with the villagers, then stalked away. Everyone snatched for whatever they could. Dien grabbed two handfuls, one a muddy brown strip, the other an old, patchy grey blanket. She pulled them close, all but snarling at the others as they hoarded their own treasures. She wrapped the grey furs around her shoulders, then gnawed on the strip, tearing it in two and wrapping the hairy furs around her feet. For the first time in weeks, she could actually feel her toes, and they hurt.

Dien watched the demons. While the pots were heated above the fires, the dead brute was strung upside down, cuts gouged into his swirling pink and black skin. Blood ran freely down the corpse and the demons gathered, letting it dribble into cupped palms then lifting it to their lips and drinking. Each one raised their head and howled to the sky after, and it seemed to Dien that every demon from both groups had a chance to drink, even those she thought were younger and with fewer horns. The brute's head was staked on a wooden pole, a bowl placed beneath it to catch any blood that dripped down. Only Swordere, the winner of the combat, was allowed to drink from that bowl.

It was some sort of ritual, Dien was sure. She thought on that. The demons had rituals, names, a language of their own. They were savages and no mistake, but they also seemed to have rules. Was there a demon society? Did they also live in villages like the humans they took as thralls?

Her da had once told her that what separated men from beasts wasn't smarts, the ability to talk or make tools. It was codes. The codes which people lived by, be it law or honour or principles. People lived by codes, both those of their society and those of their own making, and that was what elevated them above wolves or bears or chickens. But if the demons lived by codes, too, then what did that make them? And could she use those rules against them to escape?

"What are you doing?" Helena asked urgently. "Stop staring. They'll notice."

A small, skinny demon with huge, unblinking eyes walked around the villagers. Dien looked down at his approach, keeping still like all the others, praying to the Moons and Sun she wasn't taken. The demon snatched up a beefy man she didn't know from the new group.

The man rose with a roar and punched the demon in the face. The demon didn't even stagger despite being smaller than the man. It brayed out a laugh and pushed the man, sending him flying. The man rolled to a stop and got shakily to his knees. The demon stalked towards him. There were others watching now, too, though none got involved.

"Fighting meat," the demon hissed in a reedy voice. "Tough meat. Fight Roka. Fight meat."

As the demon came close, the burly villager surged up again with a thunderous punch. The demon caught the man's fist and twisted. There was a sickening crack as his arm snapped. He fell down, mewling.

"Fighting meat," the demon brayed. "Fight Roka. Fight Roka." But the man had no more fight left in him.

The demon who Dien thought was called Roka reached down and grabbed the wounded villager by his broken arm. He screamed as he was dragged away to be slaughtered for the pots.

Dien raised her head and went back to watching the macabre celebration. Some of the demons fought each other in a circle of their brethren. None were killed as far as Dien could tell, but the fights were brutal things that always ended in spilled blood. Other demons stabbed little bone needles into each other over and over. The brute's body was finally cut down and sliced up, parts distributed into only three of the pots. The burly villager was similarly butchered, his body given to the other three pots. Dien studied it all, even as all the others tried not to. She needed to understand the demons, to know what codes they lived by.

That night, as the Blood Moon alone rose into the sky, the demons ate their own and fed the villagers their own. Dien pushed her bowl away as soon as it was dropped before her, not caring who snatched it up. She dug in the dirt, ripping up grass until she found worms and crawlers. She shared her meagre bounty with Helena, but they both went hungry even as the rest of the villagers ate heartily. There were no others holding out anymore, only the two of them.

After feeding, the humans lay down to sleep on the cold, hard ground. There was nothing else to do. Dien forced herself to stay awake for as long as she could, sitting with her new furs wrapped around her, almost warm for the first time in so long. She studied the demons cavorting and howling in the firelight until her eyes drooped closed.

CHAPTER 5

Morning arrived too soon and it became clear the two bands of demons had become one. The two groups of villagers were merged, and though Dien was still tied to both Helena and the trader, Samir, she recognised few other faces among her new group except for the disapproving grimace of Enna Rusk.

Dien had never really known Enna. The woman was five years her senior and had few friends among the adults of Berrywhistle. Everyone agreed it was her domineering manner that put folk off, men and women alike. It didn't matter how wise or learned another was, Enna always had to be right. Despite that, Dien found she respected the woman's fire and determination.

Grey clouds gathered in the lightening sky and the first fat flakes of snow fell. The demons changed direction, driving the villagers south straight towards the mountains at a more determined pace than before. It was rough going, especially with Roka, the skinny demon who never seemed to blink, taking a special interest in any who walked too slowly.

Dien watched the demons whenever she could. The two bands had merged so easily. She'd expected aggression, fighting.

"I don't understand," she said as they crunched through a thin layer of snow that chilled her feet even through the new furs. "I thought the demons were always fighting."

"They are," trader Samir whispered over his shoulder. He was looking leaner these days, much of his flesh burned away so the skin around his chin was wobbly. His hair grew in a bushy, wild horseshoe around his head. "Or they were. Before."

Dien sped her pace a little until she was just a step behind the trader. "But there was so little fighting. I expected the two clans to clash. They are two clans?"

"Not anymore." The trader sighed. "Used to be that's exactly what would have happened. Two raiding bands from different clans meet, slaughter each other until only one clan remains. The giant demon changed all that. He's united all the clans."

"How do you know this?"

"Rivern has been sending scouts south over the mountains for years. Best way to keep track of demon raiding bands. Summer past, one of our scouts came limping back to the village. She was dying, cut up and bleeding. Said the other three scouts she'd gone out with were all dead. Told us about this giant of a demon, tall as two of me, riding a monstrous beast like a demon bear. This giant gathered all the clans, killed the leaders, one after another, in brutal fights. Told the demons they were united against the foe."

"The foe?" Dien asked. "Us?"

Roka stormed past, lashing his hairy whip back and forth. "Walking meat." Dien caught a lash on her arm that made her fingers numb. She felt blood trickling down her elbow, soaking into her grimy rags. She dropped back from the trader and fell silent until Roka had walked on, then slowly closed the gap again.

"The foe is us?" Dien whispered.

The trader's shoulders rose and fell in a shrug, but he didn't look back at her. "I guess. Don't really make sense though. Things changed after the giant took charge. When bands from different clans meet, they don't slaughter each other no more. The leaders fight. The losers are absorbed into the winner's clan."

"No more slaughtering each other."

"Aye. Then they came charging out of the pass. More and more of them. Beyond counting. Never thought so many demons could exist. That's when the Adjudicator of Rivern sent all us traders out, to warn as many villages as we could. Too late. These newcomers are from Sireridge, that's far to the north. If the demons have spread that far already…" He fell silent and his shoulders slumped.

"They're taking us somewhere. They don't just mean to kill us or they wouldn't have bothered giving us furs. They mean us to survive. Where are they taking us?" Dien asked.

"Mountains. Thrall pens."

"Thrall pens. Why?"

The trader glanced over his shoulder and there was despair in his eyes. "Demons are strong, but they're lazy, too. They'll work us 'til they can't no more."

"We have to escape."

He laughed bitterly.

"You said the scouts Rivern sent used to watch the demons. It must be possible to evade them, remain hidden. If we can escape…"

"I'm no scout, girl. I'm just a trader. Old and fat."

"You're not fat anymore," Dien said with a grin.

The trader chuckled, a real laugh without bitterness. He plucked at his faded, ruin of a shirt that had once been so bright and fine and colourful. "No. I suppose I'm not no more."

Behind Dien, Helena grunted as Enna Rusk tugged on the rope binding them together. Helena staggered back a step and pulled Dien with her. Roka paced past again, his eyes wide and unblinking.

It took them three days to reach the mountains and the snow didn't stop. The days became nightmares of trudging through ankle deep drifts, each footstep sending icy knives into Dien's soles until her feet went numb. The nights were even worse. All the villagers huddled closer for warmth and Dien found herself sandwiched between Helena and a man she didn't know who kept trying to touch her no matter how many times she slapped his hand away. The second night, trader Samir shoved the man away and took the space at Dien's back. He did not try to touch her.

The land started to rise, making each step a little harder. The food she and Helena could scavenge became scarcer, the bugs hiding away from the snow, the soil too frozen to dig for worms. Dien's stomach clawed itself into a knotted ball of agony.

She found her mind drifting as she walked, remembering meals from back home. Sitting around a table with her parents, sharing bug bread and cold salted venison from the stores. Her da telling the same old jokes that always made Dien laugh no matter how many times she heard them. So many times he'd thump the table hard enough to make the bread rolls jump, and he'd gasp and say, *"You didn't grind them well enough, this one is still alive."*

Or the special occasions like trader visits when the Adjudicator would allow a small, controlled fire, and they would cook some of Old Swiff's chicken eggs in one of the ancient metal pans. There were even rarer times when a wild boar was spotted in the forest and the hunters managed to catch it. Each of them only got a small strip of the boar, but the taste was glorious. It was meaty and rich, tearing apart between the teeth.

Dien stared down at the bowl of villager stew that night. She could see a couple of chunks of meat bobbing in the bloody broth. She remembered the taste of wild boar. She was so hungry. The bowl was halfway to her mouth when Helena's hand fell on her leg. Dien paused and glanced across at her friend. Helena's bowl sat untouched before her, but Dien could see the question in her friend's eyes. *Can we give in? Can we eat now?*

The memory of wild boar fled and Dien was staring down at a bowl that had recently been a woman she had known. Pertwin Tivers, Aren Tivers' wife, who helped him build the oven fire each day and spread every rumour, gossip, and hearsay like a plague throughout the village. She'd loved to dance and every time there was a celebration she dragged up partner after partner to join her until Aren got jealous enough he stopped sulking and danced with her.

Dien placed the bowl on the snowy ground and pushed it away. Enna Rusk was the first to reach for it. Helena pushed her own bowl away and stared at it miserably as one of the new villagers from Sireridge snatched it up and slurped noisily.

From afar, the mountains had looked imposing. Up close they seemed impossible. They stretched on and upwards forever and were so steep they almost seemed sheer. But there was a trail leading up, full of broken rocks, narrow ledges, and pockmarked with dark, forbidding caves. And all of it covered in the steadily falling snow.

The demons moved among the villagers, snarling at them as they cut the ropes that bound them to each other. Dien's wrists were still tied together, only a short stretch allowed between them, but she could finally move freely from Helena and trader Samir.

Swordere stalked about, his whip coiled around his waist. The demon used his black sword as a walking stick, poking the snow before each step. He had a new horn erupting from his scalp, the sore around it bleeding and ugly. Had it grown there? Dien hadn't noticed it before, but now it seemed impossible she hadn't seen it growing earlier.

"No run. Running meat. Dead meat. No run. Climb now. Follow now. Climbing meat."

That first day on the mountains was the most gruelling yet. Dien quickly discovered the furs wrapped around her disintegrating sandals were not up to the task and her soles were bloody and torn by the sharp rocks hiding beneath the snow. She fell multiple times, skinning knees and palms, but always got back up. Onwards she slogged. Onwards and upwards, driven forwards without mercy. Yet she never stopped looking for a way to escape.

Every time they came upon a cave, one of the demons would approach and sniff at the entrance. Then they would either move on or stand in front of the dark portal until all the villagers had passed. It wasn't until one man tried to run that they discovered why.

Dien didn't know the man. He was one of the newcomers from Sireridge, a young man with ropey arms and a broken nose. As he trudged across the cave's mouth, he leapt from the line of villagers and ran into the darkness. None of the demons gave chase, but they all stopped to watch.

Swordere sauntered in front of the cave and turned to face the villagers. They had all stopped, Dien included. For a moment that stretched on and on, nothing happened. Then started the screaming. A bloodcurdling howl of terror from deep within the cave. Worse was when the screaming stopped and the man's wails turned to cries of terror and pleas for help.

Swordere spoke loudly even as the man still pleaded. "No run. Running meat. Dead meat." He turned to the cave. "Soon dead. First pain." They were all whipped back into motion. The man was still pleading as they walked away, but Dien thought she heard something else echoing from inside the cave. A noise somewhere between a crunch and the skittering of uncountable legs. It both terrified her and gave her heart to know there were things in the mountains even the demons feared. Perhaps whatever lived in the caves was the foe the demons were aligning against? She wondered if she could learn to discern which caves were safe and which were not.

The snow only grew thicker as they climbed, the pass more clogged until they were wading through knee deep drifts. Dien and Helena gave up walking alone and clung to each other. Even so, Dien wasn't ready for it when Helena pitched to the side and collapsed against the cliff wall. She scrabbled there, trying to get back to her feet.

"Come on," Dien hissed. She crossed over to Helena and grabbed her arm, trying to haul her back up.

"Wait!" Helena wrenched her arm free and flailed at the cliff face.

The line of villagers trudged by behind them. Then Dien saw Roka stalking forwards, eyes wide and unblinking despite the cold and snow blasting into his face.

"Get up, Helena." She pulled at her friend again.

"Leave me alone!"

"Up!" Dien hauled her friend to her feet just as Roka arrived, uncoiling his hairy whip.

"Stopping meat." He licked his chapped lips. "Eating meat." He raised his hand, the whip flying back.

Dien pushed Helena on in front of her and bowed her head, following. She felt the whip lash her back and for a few moments, there was no pain. Then it was like fire burning and freezing her flesh all at once. She cried out, bit her lip, staggered on. Blood trickled down her back, freezing her tattered rags to her skin beneath the patchy furs.

Roka rushed alongside them, his whip trailing. He moved in close, panting and snuffing, grinding his sharp teeth. Dien kept her head down, kept walking, prayed to the Moons and Sun that Helena would do the same.

When neither of the girls stumbled again, Roka growled, snapped his teeth, and stalked away. Dien sobbed. No tears, only pent-up terror she couldn't hold on to any longer, mixing with the rage and scorn she directed at the demons. She moved alongside Helena and huddled close. Her friend was clutching her arm tightly to her chest, but Dien couldn't see any injury.

"Don't fall again," Dien said. "We can't give Roka a reason."

Helena shot her a brief smile and a wink, and then staggered on through the snow without explanation. Confused, Dien forged on after her.

That evening, as the sun dropped below the horizon, the demons ushered the villagers inside a cave. They went with trepidation, the memory of the man's screams from earlier still so clear in Dien's mind. The demons lit smaller fires deeper within the cave and scooped snow into the pots to melt. Dien and all the others were left nearer the cave mouth. They were paid so little attention. They could have run there and then, but she knew they wouldn't make it far on the mountainside in the dark and cold. The demons knew it too.

Another of the villagers from Sireridge was taken, an old man with pale eyes and a tremble so bad Dien was surprised he'd made it so far. He didn't cry out once as the demons took him, nor when they murdered him. As she stared down at the steaming bowl of him, broth bloody brown and still pink chunks floating within, her will wavered again. She was so tired, so cold, so hungry. Her stomach twisted and she felt broken inside. All the others were eating, had given in long ago. Only Dien and Helena were holding out now. Even Luci, sitting in another group was slurping at her bowl. Dien found her mind so fuzzy she couldn't even remember why she was resisting.

"Here," Helena whispered, shoving something into Dien's lap.

It took Dien a few moments of staring to realise what she was seeing. Eggs. Two eggs, each one as large as her fist. She glanced over to see Helena with an egg in her own lap.

"I found them," Helena said, smiling. "Wedged in a crack, buried in a nest of twigs and fur."

"You didn't trip earlier. You were digging them out."

Helena grinned.

"You are a lifesaver!" Dien lurched to the side and planted a kiss on Helena's cheek.

"Urgh, get away," Helena said with a chuckle. "Your breath stinks."

Dien shoved her thumb into the top of one egg, cracked it open and ripped the shell away. Inside was a soup of goo with a small pale lizard floating in the centre. A little life to trade for her own. She brought the egg to her lips, slurped at the goo and then tipped the little lizard into her mouth, swallowing it before she could taste it. It didn't work. No sooner had she forced it down, she had to clamp a hand over her mouth to stop from retching. She imagined it was what congealed mucus tasted like. Still, as soon as she had control of her stomach, she gulped down the rest of the goo and broke the egg apart, licking every drop she could from the shell.

"I take it back," Dien said, still struggling to keep it down. "Not a lifesaver. You're obviously trying to kill me." She cracked open the next egg and paused.

Helena had eaten her lizard, too. She was watching Dien. She had found three eggs and had given two to her. It took great effort to hold the egg out to Helena.

"We'll split it," Helena said with a brief, gooey smile. She gulped at the egg, then handed it back. "You eat the lizard. I can't... I can't force another."

"Not exactly wild boar, is it?"

Helena shook her head. "Or pheasant. Or chicken or dear. I'd even take bug bread right now." She smiled again. "Remember Miss Trudie's squirmer cakes?"

Dien nodded. "With a dollop of Yona Yolk's skyberry preserve on top."

"That's what it is. Ignore the scales and think of pancakes."

Dien smiled at her friend's good cheer. She clenched her stomach and upended the egg, swallowing the little lizard. It slid down her throat slowly and she thought of pancakes. Then she handed the egg back to Helena who cleaned it out, licking every bit of shell.

"Mmm," Helena said, screwing her eyes shut. "I can really taste the skyberry."

Afterwards, they lay down together to sleep. Dien's stomach roiled and gurgled and ached, but her head was a little clearer. She wrapped her arms around Helena and pulled her close to share body heat.

"Thank you," she whispered into her friend's ratty nest of hair. "Thank you." And then she cried for the first time since Berrywhistle.

The next day, the snow stopped falling. It didn't make the going any easier, the passes were already clogged thick with powdery white drifts that hid everything, but the weather was no longer an oppressive thing trying to throw them back down the mountain.

The demons were relentless, wading through the snow as if it were no barrier at all. They did not seem to feel the cold, and if any of them stubbed their toe or lanced their foot on a rock, they did not show any pain.

Onwards, they climbed. Onwards and upwards through a winding, circuitous route. Donnel Ocha and another man had been chosen to pull the cart that day, but they struggled to move it through the snow. Eventually Swordere pulled them away from it and took over. The demon showed no signs of strain, easily hauling the cart through the snow. Dien watched in fascination. They had truly never stood a chance against such immense, indomitable strength. She spotted her da's hammer wedged between two crates and had the urge to run forward and grab it, to swing it at the demon's face.

They camped that night in another grim cave dripping with moisture. There was a musty smell to it, but it was soon chased away by the fires. No villager was sacrificed that night. One of the demons sent deep into the cave came back to the fires waving something in the air. Then a pack of the demons set off into the darkness. A while later they returned with arms full of mushrooms. The demons cheered.

Dien stared down at the mushroom broth. Helena waited beside her, almost as though asking for permission. It had been cooked in the same pot as the butchered villagers, served in the same bowls. In the end, Dien found her principles only held so firm before they bent. She raised the bowl to her lips and drank deeply. She had never liked mushrooms, but now she considered it the best meal she'd ever eaten. Certainly better than raw lizard egg.

On the fifth day in the mountain, they climbed through the clouds. It was treacherous going, unable to see more than two paces ahead. Again the demons strode ahead with confidence. The villagers were slower. Dien had to fight the urge to cling to Helena. If she fell, she would not be responsible for dragging her friend down with her.

Then they were through the clouds and up to the first of the major peaks. Dien staggered at the sight. She had always known what mountains were. Her da had told her they were like hills that went on for somewhere seeming like forever. She had seen them every time she had ventured to the edge of the forest, though she knew now those were different mountains. But she had never imagined they could be so tall and somehow stretch on forever. And this one, that had been so arduous to climb, appeared to be one of the smallest peaks.

Before them stretched weaving, climbing, falling mountains as far as the horizon and no doubt further still. Snow turned many of them white, while others were oddly black or grey. The clouds drifted in lazy, patchy patterns beneath them, and through it, down in brief valleys, Dien could see the green haze of trees that were hardy and defiant enough to survive the cold. It was beautiful in a frigid kind of way.

"It goes on forever," Dien said in wonder.

"Not quite," Samir whispered. "Turn around."

Dien did so. The villagers were still trudging up the trail behind her, but beyond them, she could see the mountains falling away to rolling, gentle hills. At the very edge of the horizon, she saw the haze of a mighty forest.

"Is that home?" Dien asked.

Samir shook his head sadly. "No. We've come too far for you to see your old forest, girl. I just thought you might want to look." He turned away and started walking. "Probably the last time you'll see it."

Dien drew in a deep breath and swept her gaze across the horizon. It was the most of the world she had ever seen before. In truth, it was more than she ever realised existed. She'd heard of other places, the Burning Lands, the Ice Plains, Black Crag, Rivern, but they were just names. Now she looked out across the world from so high up and realised how big a place it truly was. Surely there had to be somewhere that was safe from the demons? If she could just get free and find it.

Roka stepped in front of Dien and jabbed her in the stomach with a finger. It felt like he'd punched right through her. Dien staggered and gasped, doubled over.

"Walking meat," Roka snapped. The demon kicked her and Dien tumbled over the rocks of the mountain top. She quickly scrabbled back to her feet and staggered on, clutching at her stomach. She had another small cut leaking into her rags, and her knees and palms were skinned again.

The demon stalked past her, snarling at another villager. Dien turned back to the view, staring down through the patchy clouds to the hills and forests beyond. She'd never imagined the world was so big, that up here on the mountain she could see so much, and still so little of it. For the first time in her life, Dien thought she understood Helena's wanderlust and desire to adventure.

Dien hurried along until she was walking next to Samir again. She hugged her ragged furs tightly against the biting wind, but it gusted around her legs and made her skin feel like ice.

"How far do these mountains stretch?" she asked through chattering teeth.

The old trader glanced down at her, then around at the nearby demons. But something had changed since they started up the mountain, none of the demons seemed to care if the villagers talked now, as long as they kept walking.

"A long, long way," he said in a weary voice. "I only have the scouts' words to go on, but my village sent people as far as they could go. Some said they walked south for half a year or more and never saw the end of the mountains." He paused and scratched at his dark beard, pulled something out and crushed it between thumb and finger. "What I wouldn't give for a knife to shave."

Dien glanced over her shoulder at Roka again. She could think of a far better use for a knife.

"There are some lowlands further south," Samir continued. "The valleys you see below, some forest and lakes. To the west there is a mighty forest that would make your old home seem like a copse, but no one we ever sent in came out again. Mostly, it's just mountains, caves, and snow." He sighed again. "And demons."

"They come from the mountains then?"

"Of course. Where else would they come from?"

"Were they always here?"

"What? I... I guess so?"

Up ahead, Swordere climbed onto a rocky outcropping overlooking a steep drop. The demon threw back his head and howled into the sky, a warbling cry that echoed through the mountains and valleys. The demon waited there even after his cry had faded, his eyes pinned on the horizon. Dien trudged past him, staring hatred and not caring if he saw her. Then she heard another cry, echoing back. Swordere laughed.

A long way to the south, dark smoke drifted into the sky. The demons grew more energetic, calling between each other with excited voices. Dien knew then, they were nearing their destination. Her journey was almost over. The thought filled her with a sick dread.

CHAPTER 6

DEMONHOLME WAS WHAT DIEN CALLED IT. NESTLED IN A winding valley between three great snowy peaks, there was a lake of crystal blue water, a dense forest of soaring pine, hundreds of dark caves pockmarking the valley walls, and a festering camp of demons. Oddly, it reminded her of home, of Berrywhistle. She had never thought that demons might live in a permanent settlement. She thought they would be nomadic, always on the move, raiding human villages, never stopping. Even stranger to her, was how the demons greeted each other with excitement, raised voices, and cheers like they were returning heroes.

The surviving villagers huddled close together as the demons of the settlement stared at them with hungry eyes set deep in mottled skin. Dien took in her surroundings as they were driven through the heart of Demonholme, and saw hollows dug out of the rock, fur set above them on sticks. That was how the demons lived, not in cabins or halls, but in the ground, protected from wind and snow by thick layers of hide.

She heard a rhythmic ringing noise and stared after it to see a huge demon stood before a roaring fire, smashing metal against metal with a hammer. She knew from her da's stories that it was a forge. Something she had never seen. Something that the village, in all her years, had never allowed for the fear it would draw the demons to them. Metal working. The huge demon lifted the black metal it had been hammering, stared at the glowing length, then thrust its searing length into a barrel of blood. Dien was pushed on by the villagers behind her before she could see any more of the forge or how it worked.

She saw a butcher with carcasses strung up on sticks, blood draining into wooden buckets. Two of the carcasses Dien recognised as animals: sheep or goats. They had already been skinned and the hide was hung up and drying. The third was human. A man whose arms had been tied to a pole above. He was sliced open down the stomach, his guts spilling out. As they passed, the man's eyes cracked open and he stared at the new thralls. The butcher noticed and went at the man with a hooked knife, peeling off a strip of skin. The poor man gagged, his head lolling, eyes rolling back. But he didn't scream. Dien wondered if he was too far gone, too lost in the pain to even cry out. She turned away from the horrific sight and trudged on.

"We have to get away," she whispered to herself.

Enna Rusk heard her. Dien wasn't sure what the other woman's expression meant, only that her eyes were wide and bloodshot. She shook her head sadly.

At the far end of the camp, pressed against a sheer rock face, were six large metal cages. The bars were made of crudely forged iron, black and rusting. There were already humans in them. They were wearing furs and some were pressed against the rocky wall, as far from the demons as possible, while others lounged against the bars, peering at the newcomers.

Swordere walked to the emptiest cage and pulled open the door. Its hinges protested. "In meat. Waiting meat. Come later. Pick meat. Working meat." He stood and held the door while ten of the villagers, Dien included, walked inside. Then the demon pushed the door shut to another shrieking squeal and moved onto the next cage, pulling the door open and shoving more of them inside.

Once all the villagers were inside the cages, Swordere snapped a few words at the other demons and they all whooped and marched away. The two demon hounds prowled closer to the cages, snarling and snuffing.

Swordere gnashed his teeth at them and the hounds spun about and charged him. One leapt at him, and the demon knocked it to the ground with a slap. The other hound barrelled into his legs and knocked him to his knees. Swordere laughed and pushed the hound away, then walked into the camp, the two hounds following on his heels, snapping at each other in play.

Dien couldn't understand it. They had been left alone. The cages weren't even locked. There was nothing to stop them. They could run. She moved to the door and set her hands against the cold iron.

"Wouldn't do that, I were you," said one of the men from the next cage over. He was leaning against the bars between their cages, hands dangling through. He didn't even look at Dien. He had skin darker than her own, matted silver hair, and an accent she had never heard before.

"Why not? They're not even locked."

He turned his head lazily and stared at her with such frank appraisal Dien wanted to hide. Instead she pushed on the cage door a little. Swordere had made moving it look so easy, but it weighed so much she could barely budge it. It squealed a little and she stopped. One of the hounds came loping back towards the cages and prowled along the bars, its scabbed flank brushing against them. Even the man in the other cage pulled back, retreating behind the safety of the metal.

"And that's why they're not locked," the man said.

"Come away, Dien," Helena said. "Just stop."

"We have to get out of here," Dien said.

Helena sighed. "We do, but not now." She pulled Dien away from the bars and then slumped down against the rocky wall at the back. "We need to rest. I'm so tired."

"She's right," Enna Rusk said. "You'll get us all killed. Stupid girl."

"Like father, like daughter," Donnel said from the next cage over. Luci was in his cage, too, but she looked away when Dien met her gaze.

"Sun and Moons, Donnel Ocha, I wish you were dead," Dien snapped.

Donnel chuckled. "Nope. Still alive. Unlike my Shilly, or my father, or all the rest of our people your da got killed, so he did."

"Ooh," the man from the other cage said, relocating to lean against the bars between them. "The fun is already starting."

"Shut it, Gartlen," said a woman in his cage. She was huddled in the corner of her cage, buried in furs. "Just let the gristle eat each other."

"Oi, you," Enna gave Dien a shove that made her stagger back into the bars. The hound snarled from outside and Dien jumped back into the middle of the cage. Enna advanced on her. "What's Donnel on about? What does he mean your da got us all took?"

"He didn't," Dien protested.

"Course he did," Donnel said smugly. He wrapped his hands around the bars that separated them. Despite the hard journey, he still looked strong. Of course he'd had no issue with eating the villager stew. "Your da were the Peace Breaker, he were. It were his evil brought the demons to us. Damned, is what it is. Cursed, just like all you Hostains."

Enna took a step back, her lip twitching in disgust. "You telling it true, Donnel Ocha? You admit it right now if you're lying."

"Not a lie on my lips, Enna Rusk," Donnel said. "As the Moons and Sun are my witness, her da were the Peace Breaker. Made a deal with the Adjudicator to keep it secret, he did, but that don't change who he were. All the Hostains are cursed, and they brought that misfortune down on us all. Still will, if we let them. Let her. Best do something about it, I say."

Dien stared at them all and found so few friendly faces. Luci looked away. Samir crossed his arms and stared at her with a frown. Even that was better than the others. The people left from her village, so few of them now, watched her with mistrust and disgust. And it wasn't just them, the villagers from Sireridge were the same, gazes like they were staring at a wild animal, wondering if it was hunter or prey.

"Yup, best do something about it," Donnel said slowly, leering through the bars.

Helena lurched back to her feet. "Don't you try it, Donnel Ocha. If you do, I'll—"

"You'll what, Helena Tressel? Go on, what'll you do?"

"I'll..." Helena glared at him. "I'll piss in your boots."

Donnel roared with laughter. Metwit joined in. "I'm terrified," Donnel said.

Helena glared at him for a few more moments, then kicked some dust his way and turned back to Dien.

The worst part of it all, was that Dien had no idea what her father had done to earn such animosity. She'd never heard the words *Peace Breaker* before. She knew her father hadn't always been a carpenter, but now she thought about it he'd never spoken about his past, at least not to her.

She remembered a time just a few years ago. A trader from the far west who claimed he lived at the edge of a lake so large it had no end came to the village. He was a whip thin man who wore coloured scarfs around his head and walked with a limp. He'd seen her da and immediately quit his cart, despite all the precious metal tools it carried. The two of them had gone inside the cabin, her da shutting the door. Dien had listened but could hear nothing but hissed whispers. Then the trader had left Berrywhistle without trading them a single thing.

Afterwards, when Dien asked about it, her da had simply said, "The past doesn't make a man, but it can break him." It seemed the past could break her, too. Only it wasn't her past at all.

Dien shuffled into the corner, where the bars met the stone cliff face. She sank down and hugged her knees tight to her chest. She didn't like the way the others were staring at her.

"We should pick her," Donnel said. "I say, next time the demons come to take one of us, throw her to them." He said it so easily. Dien glared at him.

"No need for that," Gartlen said. "You're safe now."

The woman buried in furs chuckled. "Safe."

Gartlen shrugged. "Safe enough. I'm guessing on the way here one of you was picked for the pot whenever they couldn't hunt up enough grub? Good way to whittle out the weak. Go too slow, in the pot you go." He laughed and Dien thought he sounded a bit mad. "Fall and don't get up, you're for the chop."

He sobered and gripped the bars. "Same rules apply here. Work when you're told. Do what you're told. Work fast enough and you'll be back in the cages, warm under all the furs you could want. Fed, too. Ain't good food, but it'll keep you moving. Do the work and live." He stared hard at Dien then. "And don't try to escape."

Samir scratched at his thicket of a beard. "What about that man we saw on the way in? Strung up, still alive as they skinned him."

"Jess is still alive?" the woman in the furs asked. She whined and buried herself even deeper in the furs.

Gartlen sighed. "That's Jess. He tried to escape."

The next morning, the demons came to put them to work. There were close to fifty humans, villagers from Berrywhistle and Sireridge, and even further away. They all had to work. The demons came in ones and twos, pulled open the gates and ordered out the villagers they wanted. Dien watched as Swordere pulled Donnel and Metwit and many of the other men away.

Gartlen informed them that the largest group was almost always for chopping wood. Demonholme had an insatiable need for wood, and much of it was later carted out, he knew not where. Once the forest in this valley was chopped down, the demons would pack up and move on to the next. It was home only for as long as it had resources to harvest. Dien wondered how long he'd been a thrall to know that, but she didn't have chance to ask.

The huge, burly demon who had been working the forge wrenched open their cage and pointed at her and Helena and Enna, then at the woman buried in all the furs from the cage over. "Work work. Forge work. Come now." They shuffled out of the cages and he pushed the door shut with a shrieking squeal of hinges.

They followed the burly demon back through the camp and Dien got a good look at the woman from the other cage for the first time. She was pale as fresh snow and had strange dark markings on her skin around her eyes and down her muscled arms. The markings were pictures of wind or water or bizarre animals, others were like the angular lines of wayfarer runes the people of Berrywhistle had carved into rocks to mark a path. She had pale blue eyes the colour of the sky after a storm, and wore furs that had been messily stitched together.

"You're from the Ice Plains, aren't you?" Dien asked as they trailed after the smith.

The woman sneered. "What gave it away?"

"The markings on your skin. My da told me your people needle ink into your flesh, but never why. That one looks like..." She reached out, pointing to a swirling mark around the woman's left eye. Quick as a flash flood, the woman reached up and snatched Dien's finger, bending it painfully. Then she let go and Dien pulled her hand back.

"You inlanders might pray to the Moons, but on the ice we worship greater things. The wind, the water, the Lords Beneath the Ice. My markings are my business, girl, and you best mind your own."

They passed the butchery. The man who had tried to run was still strung up, his guts pooling in a bucket below him, flies buzzing all around. His head lolled, but his lips twitched in a regular rhythm. He was still alive.

"Jess?" the Ice Plains woman said. She broke from the line and ran to him. "Jess, it's me. Karta. I'm here, love."

Before Karta could reach the strung-up man, a flap of cloth covering the ground was flung aside and the butcher ambled from beneath. He was a wiry demon with dark skin mottled with blue and red. A great taloned hand wrapped around Karta's neck and lifted her. She choked, spluttered, her eyes locked on Jess. His eyes opened just for a moment, then closed again.

The burly smith turned, knocked Helena down without even noticing, and stormed over. "No meat. Forge working. Mine now. Work now."

The butcher tossed Karta aside and stepped forward to meet the burly demon. They faced off, snarling at each other, while Karta, coughing and with a hand on her neck, crawled towards Jess.

Dien stooped and helped Helena back to her feet. "I think I've had enough adventure, Dien," Helena said, wincing and forcing a smile. "Do you think we can go home now?"

"There is no home," Enna snarled. "It's gone."

"You think I don't know that?" Helena snapped.

"Home sounds good," Dien said, trying to calm the two of them. "A nice warm bed, a soft pillow."

Helena turned from Enna and threaded her arm through Dien's. "The smell of oil as my father prepares the torches. I miss it."

Karta had almost reached Jess when the smith shoved the butcher aside. He grabbed Karta by the leg and dragged her through the dirt back towards the rest of them. They walked the rest of the way to the forge in silence.

The forge was under a roof of aged logs held aloft by metal poles. A blanket of old, furless leather was hung from the logs and could be repositioned to whichever side the wind was blowing from. Dien was grateful for that at least. She couldn't remember the last time she hadn't felt the biting chill of the wind. The forge itself reminded her of the kilns back in the caves at Berrywhistle. It was a rounded well of rock with a domed roof. A chimney rose through a hole in the roof for smoke to escape, and the forge was open on one side. Dien saw it was filled with dark rocks. On the other side of the forge was a huge set of bellows with wooden paddle handles large enough to stand on, and a skin of tough leather. Dien had seen a small set of bellows before, the type of person could hold easily in their hands and pump to stoke a fire, but this was many times the size.

The smith demon pointed to the bellows and grunted. "Pump pump. More heat. Work now." He picked up a shovel and scooped up some more rocks, dumping them into the forge.

Karta moved without hesitation. She pulled Enna with her and took her place on one side of the bellows, hissing at Enna to stand next to her.

"You two on that side," Karta said. "No. You, Hostain girl, stand on the outside opposite me. You're bigger and the outside is harder work. Your little friend stands next to you. There's a trick to it if you don't want to pull your shoulder out." She spat on the cold ground. "Frost take me, I can't believe the bastard lumped me with three of you gristle. Watch me and do as I do."

Karta hooked one foot around the bottom of the lower paddle, and rested her other on top so she was standing on it. Then she reached up and wrapped her hands around the upper paddle. She heaved on it, pulling down with her hands and up with her feet at the same time. With just her working it, the paddle barely shifted.

"More heat. Pump pump," the smith shouted from the other side of the forge.

Karta grunted. "Now. With me. Match my rhythm."

Enna lined up beside Karta and Dien stepped up opposite her on the bellows. She hooked her foot and reached up. Helena took position beside her. She looked miserable, but there was nothing Dien could do. Gartlen had said they were safe from the pot as long as they worked, so they had to work.

"On me," Karta said. She counted down and then heaved. They all heaved with her. Dien felt her shoulders strain and pop from the effort, her back twinged in protest, her hip ached. They dragged the paddle down once, all of them growling from the effort, and then eased off and let it inflate, dragging air in from a valve near Enna that stirred her scraggily hair.

"And again," Karta said. "Don't relax. Find the rhythm or it will break you." Just as the bellows reached full inflation, she tensed up and heaved on it again. Dien copied her, feeling her body explode with pain at the effort. Helena was slow, missed the moment, and Dien couldn't do enough to compensate. The paddle dragged down unevenly.

The smith stalked around the forge, a pair of black metal tongs in hand.

"We're working," Karta growled between breaths. "Pump pumping. No more mistakes."

The smith grunted and scratched his tongs down his back, then turned and walked back to the forge.

"He's kinder than most, but you won't get another warning," Karta said, her voice strained. "Do it right this time or he'll burn you. Now heave."

They all heaved, pulling with their arms and legs, and the paddle came down smoothly. Beside Dien, Helena sobbed as the bellows inflated.

"Get your little friend under control or she won't last the day," Karta growled.

They heaved down again and Dien had to drag harder to make up for Helena while she panted unevenly past the sobbing. Once the bellows was inflating again, Dien gasped in a breath.

"Helena, I'm sorry, but you don't have time. Stop sobbing. Just breathe. Breathe."

It was the most gruelling day of labour Dien had ever experienced and made the endless days of marching almost seem a fond memory. Things were easier when they hit the rhythm, but not by much. Occasionally the smith would call a stop, to let the fires of the forge cool a little, but it never lasted long and it seemed a mighty struggle to get the bellows working again when he roared at them for more heat.

It was around half-sun when the smith called for a longer break. Karta stepped off the bellows and whined as she stretched her arms above her head. "Rest," she said. "But don't let yourself seize up or it will be harder to start again."

The smith lumbered into the back of the forge with them and dropped a cloth-wrapped package on the ground, then he pulled over a hefty wooden barrel and sat on it, staring at them all. Karta hurried over to the cloth and unwrapped it. There were chunks of cooked meat inside. The Ice Walker picked up one and handed it to the smith. The demon bit into the steak and set to chewing with an open mouth. Karta took another chunk of meat for herself and retreated to gnaw on it. Enna Rusk waited only a moment before running forwards and snatching her own steak. Dien stared down at the meat, her stomach grumbling and twisting itself into knots.

"It's goat," Karta said around a mouthful.

"Shaggy meat. Eat now. Work soon," the smith said in a lazy voice.

There were two steaks left and Dien retrieved them both, handing one to Helena. She was sitting on the floor, hunched over, with her eyes closed, but she roused when Dien waved the meat under her nose.

"Oh, I'm so tired, Dien," Helena said.

Dien sat next to her friend. "No different from milling bugs," she said with false cheer. "Easy work really."

Helena sulked. "Easy with your freakish shoulders, maybe." She gnawed off a chunk of meat and her eyes went wide. "Moons and Sun that's good."

It was the first meat she'd had since leaving Berrywhistle and Dien tore into it, not caring that it was woefully overcooked and chewy as old leather.

They ate in silence while the smith watched them with dark eyes. After finishing the goat, Dien pulled Helena up and made her stretch out her aching back and limbs. Helena protested and squealed in pain, but she didn't stop.

Eventually, the smith stood and yawned. "Work now. Pump pump. More heat." He tore the lid off the barrel he had been sitting on and Dien saw it was filled with blood.

"What's that for?" Dien asked.

"No talking," the smith said. "Work now." He lifted the barrel and carried back through to the forge. Dien crept to the side and peered through into the forge where the smith was busy sorting through chunks of metal. In the corner of the forge, leaning against another barrel, she spotted her da's hammer. It was dusty and spotted with rust, but its simple presence helped Dien find new resolve. A piece of her da had followed her, was here with her.

"Dien," Helena hissed. "Get back here now."

Getting started on the bellows a second time was agonising and every muscle in Dien's body screamed in protest. Whenever the smith called for a brief break, she crept through to the front of the forge and peered in at the demon working. He was chiselling designs into a metal blade, then he took the glowing metal, still hot from the forge and plunged it into the barrel of blood. Her gaze kept drifting over to her da's hammer. She longed to hold it, to swing it.

They worked until long after night had fallen and trudged back to the cages without an escort. A quiet part of Dien's mind told her it was the perfect time to slip away and run, but she barely heard that voice. She was too tired. Too exhausted to run. All she wanted to do was sleep.

The bug-eyed demon Roka was at the cages, handing out bowls of broth. Dien and the others walked inside, each taking a bowl. Helena collapsed into a ball at the back of the cage, already sobbing as she buried her head in her hands, her bowl of stew forgotten. Enna limped to the other corner and leaned against the bars, slurping at her bowl. They were all stiff, their arms, legs, shoulders, and stomachs aching from the effort, their hands blistered from pulling on the bellows.

Dien sniffed at the bowl. It was earthy, full of mushrooms and reeds. She knelt by Helena and pulled her friend's hands away from her face. Helena stared at her with sunken eyes.

"We're going to die," Helena whispered. "We're going to work and work and work until we can't. And then they'll eat us. We're going to die." She sobbed again. "What's the point, Dien? What's the point of going on? It'd be easier just to get it over with."

Dien pulled Helena close, held her tight despite the burning ache in her arms. It matched the fiery anger flooding through her veins with every beat of her heart. She didn't like the despair in her friend's voice.

"Here," she said, holding the bowl up to Helena's lips. Her friend just stared blankly at it until Dien wedged the bowl in her mouth and tipped. Then she slurped it down. "Just keep going, Helena. Survive. I'll find us a way out, I promise. I'll get us out of here. Just don't give up."

CHAPTER 7

WORK. EAT. SLEEP.

Life became a gruelling routine to Dien that left her little time or energy to consider how she might escape. Demons came to the cages almost as soon as the sun breached the mountaintops, and the humans were regularly worked until long after the sun had fled the chasing moons. The only respite from the drudgery was when she was chosen for different jobs.

She was bigger than most of the other women and broader around the shoulders. Working the bellows soon put muscle on her lanky frame. After a few weeks, Swordere sometimes chose her to chop down trees with the men. She harboured fantasies of turning her axe on her captors and burying the head in Swordere's horned face, but they were only fantasies. Even if she could do it before the demon stopped her, the others would tear her apart, and then what good would she do? She needed to be smart, not rash.

Helena struggled and some days Dien was sure she was the only thing keeping her friend going. On those bad days, Helena barely spoke, and cried herself to sleep. Even wrapped in furs, she shivered and Dien pressed herself close to share her body's heat, wrapped her arms around her and held her tight. She would not allow her friend to give up, even when the darkness seemed too heavy to bear.

Tearing down the forest was a laborious process. First they had to chop down the trees and drag them away to be sized and cut. Then the roots needed digging from the earth. Despite this, of all the work she was assigned, cutting down the trees was the best. She liked swinging an axe. The rough weight of a weapon in her hands made her feel less powerless. The impact as the axe head bit into the tree was a satisfying vibration. Her blisters swelled, popped, swelled again. Then she grew callouses as thick as those on her feet. She grew stronger. Dien knew she'd never be as strong as Donnel or Samir, and certainly never strong enough to challenge even the smallest of the demons, but at least she stopped feeling so weak and pitiful all the time.

They had plenty of furs to try to keep themselves warm. The demons didn't seem to feel the cold at all. Some wore tunics like Swordere's screaming faces, but most only wore stained britches. The furs were dumped in with the humans so none of them froze during the cold nights before their usefulness had run out.

Dien managed to swipe a few bones from the butcher while the demon wasn't watching, there were always bones lying around after animals had been skinned and chopped. She hoped none of the bones had belonged to Jess. He'd survived for five more days, a full week before succumbing. Dien hadn't known him at all, but Karta cried angry tears the day he died. She took no comfort from anyone and glared at Dien when she tried to offer condolences. A tough woman made of hard lines and sharp edges.

Dien shaved the small bones down into needles and Helena set about sewing some of the furs into clothing. She worked for hours, after the sun had fled and the food was devoured, often until her hands were bloody. Dien tried to help, but she simply wasn't made for sewing.

"You have the most manly fingers of any woman I've ever seen," Helena said after Dien snapped her first needle, skewering her thumb. "All clumsy fumbling and power over finesse. You have to work the needle through, not just shove it."

Dien sucked on her bleeding thumb. "Not manly," she sulked. "Just not as dainty as you."

"You're a clumsy oaf, Dien Hostain, always have been," Helena grinned at her. "Luckily, you have me and I'm artfully delicate and... ow!" She pulled away a bleeding thumb.

"You deserved that," Dien said, thumb still in her mouth.

Helena sucked on her thumb, too. "I did."

It was crudely done, but at least the two of them said goodbye to their fraying dresses before they fell apart completely. They passed the needles on so others could make their own clothes. Donnel demanded Luci sew him a set and she gave in. Dien wanted to break through the bars and smack the bastard over the head, but there was nothing she could do, and nothing she could say. The others were still wary of her after his naming her father the Peace Breaker. She had yet to find out what that meant.

Every time she thought of her parents the grief filled her lungs, making it hard to breathe. But there was more than just grief, there was anger, too. Anger at the demons, yes, but not just them. Dien found she was angry at her da, even hating him a little. For the secrets he kept, and for not fighting back. She hated him for not surviving, for not being there for her now when she needed him most.

Once every five days, the demons pulled all the humans from the cages and marched them to the far side of the lake to bathe. Dien was thankful for that even as she understood why. The humans were thralls, there to work. The demons didn't want them getting sick while they still could be used.

The water was icy and Dien had to brace herself and walk into the gently lapping waves before her courage could give out.

The first time was the worst. Many of the thralls waited at the edge of the lake, tested the freezing waters with their toes and then backed away. Helena was one of them. Dien was up to her ankles by the time she looked back to see her friend hesitating, clutching at her dress.

"Come on," Dien said through chattering teeth. "It's not too bad."

"That's a lie, Dien Hostain. It's a bold faced lie and you know it,"

Helena said. She crept forward and poked her toe into the water again, then pulled back shaking her head. Most of the others were already in the water, washing themselves down. A few of the thralls, all newcomers, hung back.

Dien waded back to shore and grabbed Helena by her arm. She was so skinny, Dien's hand wrapped all the way around her wrist. "You're filthy, Helena. We all are. Either you bathe or you get sick."

Helena sulked. "If we're filthy, maybe they won't want to eat us."

Dien grinned. There was nothing else for it.

"Don't you dare, Dien!" Helena said and tried to back away.

Dien advanced on her friend in silence.

"Don't you dare. Don't you dare."

Dien dipped down, grabbed Helena, and tipped her over her shoulders. Helena squeaked in panic and thrashed about, but Dien held her tight, surprised at just how light her friend was. She waded back into the icy lake while the other thralls watched, some of them cheering.

"Put me down. Put me down. Put me down! Dien Hostain, if you do this I'll... I'll put squirmers down your furs at night."

Dien toes squelched in the stony mud below the surface. Oddly the water didn't feel quite so cold when she had something else to focus on. She was all the way up to her hips when Helena finally stopped struggling.

"Still want me to put you down?" Dien asked.

"No! Sun and Moons, this is going to be cold, isn't it?"

"Brace yourself."

Helena whined.

Dien heaved Helena off her shoulders and threw her straight into the lake with a thrashing splash.

Helena came up spluttering, red faced, and looking like a drowned cat. She slapped the water, then flung a cupped handful at Dien. "Oooh, you are such a... a... a slug, Dien! It's freezing."

Dien couldn't help but grin. It might have been a harsh thing to do, but it was the most energetic she had seen Helena for so long. She laughed and Helena smiled. Then Helena leapt at her and knocked her over, and then both of them were underneath the water. The cold was a shock and Dien gasped. When she came up again, she was spluttering. But she still couldn't keep the smile from her face. Some of the other thralls were laughing, too. They spent a few more seconds throwing water at each other, but soon relented. Helena wasn't lying about the cold and the sooner they washed and got back to dry land, the happier they'd all be.

After that, Karta taught the other women how to braid their hair into tight coils that would stop any of the crawlers from burrowing in and making a nest there. Dien hated having her hair bound so, but it was preferable to the alternative.

There was no privacy at the lake, the men and women washing together. More than once, Dien caught Donnel or Gartlen or one of a dozen others leering at her. Far more often, they stared at Luci and after the third bath in the icy cold, Dien pulled the little woman away from the others and into her cage. She did not trust leaving Luci alone with Donnel and his friends at night. Besides, it felt good to have both her friends by her side again.

They reminisced at night, once the moons were high and the demons were away in the camp. Stories of back home, adventures they had all shared that had seemed so exciting at the time. It was a small comfort, but it kept their spirits up. It kept Helena from succumbing to the darkness that often seemed to sour her mood and steal away her strength.

Of all the jobs the thralls had to work at Demonholme, those in the caves were the worst for Dien. It was partly the lack of daylight, everything lit by the grimy light of an oil-soaked torch, but that wasn't all. She did not like the feeling of having rock all around her. It made her feel trapped in a way even the cages didn't, like the walls were steadily closing in. She often found herself breathing hard and unable to stop a sick panic from creeping in. It was easier when she had someone to talk to. When the demons allowed them to talk. Most of the bastards were lenient enough as long as the work was done, but Roka was different. The bug-eyed demon snarled and screamed and beat them whenever the thralls talked amongst themselves.

The valley was pockmarked with hundreds of caves all up the rocky walls. Some were shallow things and others seemed to go on forever, digging deep into the bones of the mountains. Some were even flooded. Oddly, in the flooded caves, Dien sometimes saw bright blue lights burning beneath the waters, sparkling ethereal glimmers like stars beneath the waves. The demons were always quick to pull their thralls away from the flooded caves, though Dien often saw them going in afterwards and returning dripping wet. She wondered was down there, beneath the water, though it didn't seem to be a way out.

There were two jobs in the caves. The first was mushroom harvesting. Expansive mushroom colonies grew large and plenty in some of the caverns, like small forests underground where no light shone. Picking the mushrooms was an easy task, spending all day crawling along the spongy, mossy floor, filling basket after basket with the things. Dien hated it for spending all day crouched made her back ache like no other job.

Helena always seemed happiest when she was picked to harvest the fungi, and Dien thought that maybe it was because it reminded her of bug picking back home. For Helena, looking back on better times made her happy. Dien found it often made her sad and angry. The reminder of the quiet, easy life that had been stolen from them made her blood boil in her veins. More than once, she ended up crushing a mushroom in her fist and felt like screaming out her frustration.

There were some mushrooms they weren't allowed to pick. Every time the demons led the thralls into the caves they pointed them out. "Grey capped. Eating food. Pick pick. Spotted yellow. No eat. No eat. No pick."

The forbidden mushrooms were always brown capped with yellow spots and they grew in particularly moist patches of the caves. They were always solitary things, only ever surrounded by grey caps. Having grown up in a forest, Dien was used to hearing about poisonous fruit or leaves or mushrooms and knew to leave well alone. Though sometimes she saw Helena staring at the spotted mushrooms, a faraway look in her eyes. Dien always pulled her friend away when she saw it, but she worried about what Helena might do when she wasn't around. It was selfish, she knew, but Dien didn't think she could keep going without Helena. She needed her friend. Needed someone to stay strong for.

The other job in the caves was mining. Dien still hated the enclosed feeling of the walls bearing in on her, but she much preferred digging out rock and ore to picking mushrooms. Just like with the woodcutting, she enjoyed having something to swing. The feel of the pickaxe striking stone, the reverberation through her arms, the sparks of light a brief but satisfying violence.

They mined in threes, two people digging out the ore and that strange rock that seemed to burn in the forge, and the other ferrying the rocks out of the cave in buckets. The demons patrolled the caves, keeping a lazy eye on all the groups of miners, though Dien was sure it was only to keep the thralls working. There was no escape through the caves, only a cold, dark death.

At night, after the thralls were back in their cages and fed, the demons cared little for what they did. Some of them simply slept, getting as much rest as possible in preparation for the next day, while others chatted, shared stories. Some even paired off and rutted in dark corners, though Dien thought them stupid for it.

It was after winter shifted into spring that Dien saw Enna slink off into a corner with Panyet. She stared after them for a few moments until Enna caught her gaze and sneered. Back in Berrywhistle, Dien had often stared at Panyet. He had always been quiet and strong and so very handsome. She had felt something for him, something she'd never really acknowledged. Helena and Luci had noticed and they never missed a chance to poke fun at Dien for her mooning.

It hadn't been too long ago, back in Berrywhistle, they'd been sitting at the mills, grinding bug flour when Panyet strolled past. He'd popped one of the seams on his shirt about the shoulders and Dien stopped to watch him go.

"Did you just drool into the mill, Dien?" Helena had asked in a dramatic voice.

Dien frowned at her but Luci joined in. "Every time with Panyet. She goes glassy eyed and slack-jawed."

"Oh, Panyet," Helena said in a high voice that was nothing like Dien. "You're so tall and manly and you have such big feet."

"Big feet?" Dien asked. She'd never paid any attention to his feet.

"It's important, trust me," Helena had said with a lurid wink. "At least, that's what my mother says."

Luci had cut in with a grunt that was a decent impression of Panyet and about as much conversation as anyone ever expected from him.

Dien had scowled at them both and they'd all laughed. "Well, he is handsome," she'd said eventually, and they'd all agreed with that.

Panyet was not handsome anymore. The demons had scarred him with two ugly wounds down his face, but he still maintained a quiet strength. Dien could not fault Enna for the choice of partner, only for the choice itself. What if she got pregnant from the rutting? How long would she be able to continue working? What would the demons do when they saw she was carrying a child?

Dien knocked on the bars to get Gartlen's attention. He still preferred to sleep in the same cage he always had, though many of the thralls switched cages whenever they pleased.

"Where are all the children?" Dien asked.

"Huh?" Gartlen had been dozing against the bars. "You want a child? Well, these bars are in the way, but if you bend over I'm sure I can..."

Dien reached through the bars and gave him a shove. He grinned at her. "The demons," she said. "I'm sure I've seen younger ones. The ones with fewer horns. But where are the children? Where do they come from?"

"They ain't like us, girl," Karta said. She still called Dien a *girl* even though Dien was a head taller than her and broader, and not much younger. "They don't have kids."

Gartlen shrugged and nodded his agreement. "I've been in this valley since the camp settled here, and I was in two others before it. Never seen a demon child. Don't think they breed. They don't need to. They just... are, I guess. Maybe they grow, like mushrooms. Angry little demon mushrooms sprouting out of the earth screaming *Pick me. Pick me.*"

Samir sauntered closer. He always kept to the same cage as Dien and

Helena and Luci. Got between them and any of the men whose hands wandered. Dien was both glad of the protection and angry that he thought she needed it. But neither Helena nor Luci had grown like she had or put on the muscle. They were both still small and thin, whereas she was clearly growing into her da's daughter.

"No scout Rivern ever sent reported children," the old trader said.

"They don't need children," Helena said sleepily. She was lying down, her head in Luci's lap. "They're immortal."

Samir nodded sagely.

"But they fight each other," Dien pressed.

"Not anymore," Samir said.

Dien shook her head. She needed to know the answer. "But where do they come from?"

"South, I guess," Gartlen said. "Beyond the mountains. Whatever is beyond these bloody peaks."

Again Dien shook her head, her braid whipping against the bars. "That's not what I mean."

"Oh stop it, Dien," Gartlen said. "Everyone knows what you mean. You want to know if they rut. If they wriggle together in horny ecstasy. Slapping each other's arses and grunting *Take meat. Take meat. Take meat.*"

"Shut up, Gartlen," Karta snapped. The Ice Plainer had no humour whereas Gartlen couldn't utter two words without joking. "One day a demon is going to tear out your tongue and cook it, and I will eat happily and enjoy the peace and quiet for once."

"Maybe so," Gartlen said with a wink towards Karta. "Then I will have to take up humming. Very loudly."

Everyone else chuckled, even Karta, but Dien's mind was still aflame with questions. In the silence that followed, they heard Enna and Panyet shifting in the darkness. There was an unspoken rule that you ignored what happened between thralls at night. One of the two moaned and Dien felt the need to drown out the noise with more words.

"They have to come from somewhere," she said sulkily.

Karta shook her head. "You think of them like us. Like humans. They ain't us."

"Well, they look a little like us."

"Speak for yourself," Gartlen said with a grin. He held up his hands when she glared at him. "I mean it. You ever seen a woman demon? By the Fire's Light, I've never even seen below their rags. Do the demons have cocks under there?"

"That bloody hound does," Samir said, thumbing over his shoulder to where one of the demon hounds dozed outside the cages.

"And two bloody great swinging balls," said Karta.

"The other one doesn't," Helena said, her head still in Luci's lap. "The one with sabrefangs is female. Looks like that wolf pup Pertwin Tivers rescued three years back. Got teats and everything." Luci stroked Helena's hair and Helena smiled closed her eyes.

If the demon hounds were male and female, it only stood to reason that the other demons were the same. And yet, Gartlen was right, there were no women demons in the camp. No demon children either.

"Besides," Gartlen continued. "You haven't seen the other ones yet. The big ones. The monsters." The smile fell from his face and he shook his head. "These ones might have our shape, but they're not human. Once you see the big ones, you'll understand."

"What does it matter anyway?" Karta said, rubbing at one of the markings inked onto her cheek. "Where they come from. Big demons, little demons. Demons with great big cock and balls. Lords Beneath the Ice, girl, none of that's gonna help you survive, so what's it matter a damn anyway?"

Dien didn't need to consider the question, she already knew the answer. Years ago, when she was still too young to work the bug mills, and too distracted to sit while her ma sewed or tended the gardens, she used to follow her da around everywhere he went. When he picked up a log, she picked up a stick. When he grabbed his hammer, she found a stone. When he built a wondrous bit of furniture, she made kindling.

He used to chat to her, always talking about what he was doing and why. Why lining up the logs and cutting them straight mattered. How to hold a chisel so the strike was clean. How to look along the grain of the wood. He told her that bit often.

"Not every log serves every purpose, little bug," he'd said. "You have to study the grain, the way the tree grew. Once you understand it, you know what its capable of. Whether it will cut straight. Will it warp as it ages? Put the knot in just the right places to strengthen the joints or the whole thing will crumble. Understanding the wood is the key to working it." She remembered the time his face went still, his eyes haunted. "Just like understanding a man is the key to destroying him."

She hadn't been old enough to know what he meant back then, still just a child. Now things were different. She was a woman grown who had seen death and worse. The world shone less vibrant. Demons were no different than wood, or whoever the man her da had talked about had been. She needed to understand them.

"What about the swords?" Dien asked. "And the axes?"

"Huh?" Samir said as he crossed his broad arms. He had put on so much muscle and looked almost a different man from the pudgy trader who had come to Berrywhistle. Still hadn't managed to shave his bushy beard or messy band of hair though. "We use the axes to chop the forest."

"Not those ones. The ones the smith makes and squirrels away. He uses blood in their forging and the blades turn out black rather than silver."

Karta scratched behind her ear, caught something wriggling, crushed it. "The ones in the barrels," she said. Karta most often worked the bellows in the forge unless another demon beat the smith to her. Many of the demons had favourites from among the thralls. "Most of the weapons the smith makes are put in barrels, then shifted to one of the pits in the ground, covered over with thick hide. Far as I know, they're kept there."

They all looked at Gartlen. He'd been there the longest, surely he had to know what it was all for. He just shrugged. "Don't look at me. I rarely get out of the mines. Pretty sure the bastards think I'm half murk."

"What's a murk?" Helena asked.

"You don't have murks where you come from?" Gartlen said and whistled, shaking his head. "Lucky you. Big as a boar and with claws as long as my arm. They tunnel through the ground. You ever see a murk, start running."

"Why?"

Gartlen smiled. "Because when they come above ground, it means the black fires are coming. Out east in the Ashlands, past the Burning Earth, you do not want to get caught in the black fires."

Dien wanted to know more about the Ashlands. Gartlen spoke of it so rarely, but she decided to drag them back on topic. "The smith is making weapons here. Weapons are made to fight. That's their only purpose. You've already said they don't fight each other anymore."

"Not since that big bastard monster of a demon united the clans," Samir said.

"So why all the weapons?" Dien asked, relentless. "Not to fight us."

"They don't need weapons to kill us," Helena said. Luci was busy stroking her hair, staring off into the darkness where Enna and Panyet were vague shapes moving against each other.

"Exactly," Dien said. "So who? Why make all those swords and axes? Who are the demons fighting? Because it's not us. They just... take us."

They all fell silent. Panyet grunted, Enna gasped. Both of them were panting in the darkness.

"Lucky bastard," Donnel's voice drifted out from the next cage over and was greeted with a round of laughter.

Dien curled up behind Helena that night, held her friend close. Luci lay down on the other side draped their fur blanket across them all. Helena was always cold, always shivering. Before she dropped off to sleep, she saw Enna Rusk creep away from where Panyet was snoring. Enna found a spot that was all her own and placed her back against the rock. She hugged her knees and cried silent tears that she thought no one else could see.

CHAPTER 8

The season turned from spring to summer. Only the lengthening days informed them so high up in the mountains, as the weather barely changed. Perhaps it was a little warmer but not enough to matter. The days rolled one into another until Dien could barely remember anything but Demonholme.

She tried to think back, to remember her life at Berrywhistle but couldn't. She knew it had been easy and pleasant, not that it had seemed that way at the time. But she couldn't remember the form of her days from so long ago. It was with no mild panic she also realised she could no longer remember her parents' faces. A betrayal to all they had done for her. The final shovel of soil over their graves. They were gone. Even her grief faded like a dress washed too many times and turned grey and lifeless. All that remained was her anger at her da for the secrets he kept, her unfair hatred that he had refused to fight and left her all alone.

The summer days were harder than the winter. The demons worked them with the light and the thralls soon came to despise the banging of claws against the bars waking them in the morning.

"Do you remember Hookstone?" Luci asked one time when they

were on mushroom picking duty together. The greasy torch was burning away in its brazier, casting them in a gloomy flickering light.

"I remember sitting on top of it with you and Helena, staring at the mountains," Dien said. "I used to think they looked so small. Like little pimples in the land."

Luci's laugh was the tinkle of water in a quiet brook. "Helena wanted to go and explore them, didn't she?"

Dien nodded and plucked another grey cap from the colony. She had learned it was important to take the adult mushrooms only and before they grew too big. Take one of the larger mushrooms and the whole colony might fail without its protection. Take them too young, and they never had chance to grow, again the colony was likely to fail.

For the first time, Dien realised there were really no children in Demonholme. Not just the demons, but the humans, too. There had been youngsters at Berrywhistle, little Ransa Owne and Isos Merry were always running around underfoot getting in the way like it was a challenge to trip up as many adults as they could, and she was certain there must have been children at Sireridge, too. Yet the demons had not taken any of them. Dien wondered if they had been left alive, a forest full of children running around with no supervision sounded both a wonderful and terrifying thing. Perhaps once they escaped, they would return and find the village rebuilt and chubby-cheeked Isos Merry in charge of the whole thing, a tiny little elder. The thought made her smile.

Dien dragged her mind back to the conversation. "Helena was always wanting to explore. Never happy at home. Said she wanted to be free to see the world."

"She doesn't want to explore anymore," Luci said quietly. In the dim light, Dien could see her friend staring down at one of the spotted mushrooms. There was always a bit of space between the spotted ones and the rest of the colony as if the other mushrooms were afraid to get too close, and yet the colonies always grew thickest around them too. It was a strange contradiction. "She doesn't want anything anymore. I'm worried about her."

"She will," Dien said, trying to force some mirth into her voice. "It'll be just like old times. Helena will be sick with wanderlust again once we..." She glanced around. Roka was lazing against a wall, his bug eyes closed for once. Dien glared at the demon a moment and then away. She wanted to say *once they escaped*, but she wouldn't utter it around a demon, not even one who appeared to be asleep. "She's just in one of her dark times. She'll pull out of it, she always does."

Dien plucked another grey cap and put it in Luci's basket while the other girl wasn't watching. It felt good to help out her friend.

"I never wanted to explore," Dien said. "Not really. I just wanted to be like my da—"

"HAH!" Metwit said with a derisive snort. "Your da was a filthy traitor brought the demons to us. Glad we killed him."

Metwit was often picked for mushroom duty. He was one of Roka's favourites. Metwit glanced up at Roka, saw the demon wasn't watching, reached into his basket and popped a mushroom in his mouth. The demons didn't like them eating anything outside of feeding time, but they couldn't always be watching. Sneaking food was one of the perks of the job.

Dien decided to ignore the beaver-faced bastard, but when she turned back to her work she saw Luci was glaring at the man with a fierce look Dien had never seen on her face before.

"I wanted to make things," Dien said to pull Luci's attention away. "Build things."

Luci blinked a few times and her expression softened. She looked down at the mushrooms below her again and crawled away from the spotted one, picked a grey cap instead.

"You wanted to be your da. Helena wanted to run away. I was the only one who wanted what was meant for me." Luci smiled wistfully. "I wanted to be an herbalist just like my mother, and I..." She paused and blushed. "I was going to marry Gragor Nuln."

Metwit chuckled.

"He took me out to Hookstone," Luci continued. "We kissed." She blushed. "We did more than kiss. I was going to marry him and start a life right there in Berrywhistle."

"You and every other girl with loose skirts," Metwit said. "Grag made a game of it. How many of you he could pound beneath the hook."

Luci was staring at Metwit again, her eyes shining in the fizzing torch light, but not from tears. There was nothing there at all. No fury, or sadness, or embarrassment. Luci stared at Metwit with cool, blank regard.

"What happened to Grag anyway?" Metwit continued oblivious.

Luci tore her eyes away from Metwit and gently picked a mushroom, placing it in her basket. "The same thing that happened to everyone. He's dead," she said it so flatly, as though she wasn't talking about the man she had just professed she was intending to marry. "I saw him die. Watched them..."

Dien reached out and patted Luci's hand where she was crushing one of the mushrooms. "It's alright."

Luci turned to her then, and Dien recoiled. The stillness in her face was terrifying. "It's not alright, Dien," she said, her voice flat and emotionless.

The torch gave a spluttering pop and sparks fizzed around them. Roka snorted, waking with a snarl. He pointed at Dien. "Fetching meat. More torch. Get light. Fetch now." He yawned, showing off a maw of fangy teeth.

Dien gave Luci's hand a squeeze, then stood. There was no arguing or disobeying Roka no matter how much she wanted to stay with her friend.

She hurried through the dark with her head down, hand trailing along the wall so she didn't get lost. She stubbed her toe on an outcropping once, stepped on sharp little rocks but barely felt it her callouses had gotten so thick. The light of day dazzled her when she finally reached the cave mouth and Dien had to shield her eyes for a few seconds until the glare died away.

Demonholme was just a short walk away, a few minutes along the valley floor. There were no demons keeping watch between the cave and the camp. No one to stop Dien from turning tail and running. She could find a trail, climb out of the valley, follow the sun west towards the forest

Samir said even the demons dare not enter. Nothing that waited within the woods could be worse than life at Demonholme, and Dien knew how to forage from the trees and animals.

Yet she knew it for nothing but a foolish dream. She wouldn't get far before Swordere and his demon hounds tracked her down. And besides, she couldn't leave Luci and Helena behind. She needed a better way to escape, one the demons couldn't track. One that could get them all out. They were probably better making their escape at night as well, so their disappearance wouldn't be noticed until much later, but the bars to the cages squealed like a gutted boar when they were opened or closed.

Dien hurried on towards the camp, keeping her head down. Thralls were often sent on errands and most of the time none of the demons bothered them unless they were seen lazing about or were foolish enough to meet their gazes. The demons seemed to take looking at them as a challenge to their strength and none were willing to overlook it.

She threaded her way in between the sleeping pits, the fires, the wood stores, and the forge. Glancing up as she passed the latter, she saw Helena working on the bellows opposite Enna. Helena had a vacant look on her face and Enna snapped at her to keep up her side of the work. Luci was right, Helena was losing hope. Dien decided she needed to do something about that.

A demon snarled at her and Dien staggered away, lowering her head again. There were hundreds of them, some working, others doing nothing but standing around snapping off brutal words in their strange language. Dien slowed and listened to them for a few moments. It was another language she was hearing and they did understand each other, yet they always seemed to speak the same language as the humans when around the thralls. Did that mean all the demons knew two languages? She wondered if it was possible to learn demon, to speak it.

When she reached the butcher, Dien waited for the demon to notice her. It was not wise to demand their attention. There was always one of the hounds lying about near the butchery, though she could never remember which of the monsters was which. This one was the bitch with sabrefangs and it yawned when it noticed her, then stood up, stretched, and padded towards her, great raking claws tapping at the rocky ground. It drew close and snuffed at her, hot, rancid breath blowing out against her neck. Dien kept her head down, clenched her hands into fists, and desperately tried to will herself to stay still. The demon hounds were so much larger than the dogs some of the traders used to bring around, so much larger than the wolves sometimes spotted in the forest. They were covered in mange and stank of carrion. They terrified her more than any of the demons apart from Swordere himself.

"Waiting meat. What want?" the butcher said, barrelling towards her. He had a black iron cleaver in one hand and his broad chest and ragged britches were stained with blood not his own. He was one of the palest demons in the camp, tall and rangy, and one of the most brutal.

"I need a new torch for the cave," Dien spat the words out, staring at the butcher's taloned feet. He had an old horn on the knuckle of his big toe that had apparently broken off and was barely hanging on by the torn skin around it. "Roka sent me. New torch."

The demon hound huffed hot breath at her neck again and Dien couldn't stop the whine that escaped her lips.

"New torch. Fresh fire," the butcher grunted and turned. "Come now."

Dien turned, shaking, to stare at the demon hound. Its lips pulled back a little, baring yellowing teeth dripping with saliva. Its breath was a reek that almost made her gag. She could never forget this monster had savaged her da's corpse and had torn apart her ma.

"I hate you," Dien hissed. She wasn't certain it couldn't understand, nor that it couldn't tell the other demons what she had said. All she knew is she put her full heart behind her words and had never spoken anything more true. "I. *Hate*. You."

The demon hound just watched her, beady red eyes in a sunken skull surrounded by rotten flesh and mangy fur. Dien hurried after the butcher, still trembling.

The butcher was round the back of the butchery where he kept the barrels. He heaved one up and dropped it in front of Dien. It was filled with a viscous oozing yellow liquid that wobbled sickeningly. A large bubble of air meandered up to the surface and sat under a greenish film. It was grease, Dien realised. The grease the butcher had harvested from all the carcasses he cut up and drained.

"New torch," the butcher said.

Dien barely heard the demon. She was staring into the barrel of grease, a plan beginning to form in her mind. The first step to their escape.

The butcher thrust the torch against her chest and roared at her, all impatient fury and no words. Dien grabbed the torch and staggered back from fright.

"New torch. Fresh fire. Slow meat. Stupid meat." The butcher chuntered to itself as it heaved the barrel of oil and then the grease barrel back into place, then closed the metal grating behind them and lowered the fur flap over the top.

Dien turned and scampered away as quickly as she could, clutching the new torch against her chest. She glanced once at the demon hound as she passed. If she could just find a way to mask their scent against the monsters, they could do it. They could escape.

Dien made it back to the cave mouth in time to hear the first blood-curdling scream echo from the darkness. She almost ran straight in, but wandering around the dark was pointless. She dropped the torch and grabbed a couple of stones, bashing them together to make a spark. It didn't catch. She tried again and again.

Another scream reverberated from the cave, filled with pain. Dien struck the stones again, harder. She opened a gash on her thumb and ignored it, kept striking. One of the sparks leapt onto the torch, still hot enough to ignite the oil. The torch flared to light and Dien dropped the stones and snatched up the burning brand, waving it towards the darkness. She saw a pair of eyes shining out at her, coming closer.

Luci stumbled from the cave mouth, her basket of mushrooms looped over one arm. She didn't look hurt or scared. She just walked out into the daylight and dodged around Dien's torch, then took up position behind her.

Roka was next out of the cave, his bug eyes wide, his mouth stretched into a wild grin that made the horns sticking out of his cheeks pull on his skin. He was laughing as though someone had just told him the funniest joke.

Metwit did not follow them. He screamed again from deep within, a noise filled with unbearable anguish.

"What happened?" Dien asked.

Luci stared at her, eyes flat and spoke in a voice just as empty. "Metwit ate a spotted cap."

Roka guffawed again, waved a hand towards the two thralls. "Back away. Back meat. Away away. Stupid meat. No eat. Spotted cap. Stupid meat." The demon shook his head and laughed.

Dien grabbed Luci by the arm and pulled her away from the cave mouth. "How?" Dien demanded. "How did he eat a spotted cap?"

Luci's flat stare was terrifying, "It must have fallen into his basket."

Metwit screamed again from inside the cave.

Swordere strode across the grassy ground towards them, the other demon hound at his side. Dien backed away from Swordere, pulling Luci with her, bowing her head. She glanced up as he passed, hated him as much as she did the hounds. Swordere's screaming face tunic seemed to stare back at her, the stretched, dark pits that had once been eyes following her every movement.

"What scream?" Swordere growled.

Roka laughed again. "Stupid meat. Eat spotted. Weak meat. Too much. Scream scream. Dead soon. Stupid meat."

Metwit screamed again, closer now.

Roka backed away from the cave mouth, still laughing. Swordere stood before it, waiting, his back straight. Dien was still holding the torch. She had the urge to rush forwards and smack Swordere around the head with it, hope the demon's patchy hair caught fire and burned him up. Another useless dream. She just needed to be unnoticed until she had a full escape plan.

Finally, Metwit careened out of the darkness, screaming. His mouth was open so far the corners had torn. There were oozing furrows down his face and his fingernails were bloody. Blood ran from his eyes and nose.

He staggered into the wall of the cave, howled in fury, and swung his fist at it. Chips of rock shattered and bounced away and two of his fingers snapped. The pain didn't seem to mean anything to him, he was so lost in it.

Metwit closed on Swordere and swung for him. The demon swayed backwards out of the way then kicked Metwit in the chest, knocking him to the ground. Before Metwit could get up, Swordere leapt forward, planted a foot on his chest, and ripped his head from his body in a gush of blood.

The demon hound stalked forward, lips drawn into a snarl as it snuffed the blood. Swordere raised Metwit's severed head, regarded it for a moment, then tossed it aside. "Bad meat. No eat. Bad meat." He bared his teeth and glared at the chuckling Roka. "Working meat. No break." He walked away without so much as glancing at Dien and Luci. "Eira come."

The demon hound crept a little closer to the bleeding body, a clicking, gurgling sound issuing from its mouth, then it turned and leapt away after its master.

Roka's laugh echoed as he walked into the cave. "Come meat. Work now. No eat."

Dien held onto Luci for a few moments longer, turned the smaller woman to face her. She was so still, her face as calm as a frozen pond. "Luci," Dien said, shaking her by the shoulders.

The smaller woman blinked a few times and sagged, her mouth turning down in disgust. "Oh, that's horrible. Poor Metwit."

"Luci, how did the spotted cap get into Metwit's basket?"

Luci clutched at Dien, holding her tight. She was trembling. "I..." She drew in a hitched breath, then tore away and ran into the cave with her hand over her mouth.

Dien stared at the body for a few more moments. She tried to find some sympathy for him but couldn't. Metwit Pa had helped murder her father. He'd been a bully his whole life, and in the absence of rule and civilised society, he'd only gotten worse. He and Donnel making allies of the biggest men sharing their cage, taking food from those smaller.

Her da had once told her: *The true measure of a man isn't what they do when life is easy, it's what they're capable of when things get hard.* But Dien was starting to think he had it backwards. The true measure was what a person was unwilling to do, no matter how tough life was. That was what defined them, what raised them above the demons. The codes they lived by, each and every one of them.

In uncivilised society, Donnel and Metwit had no low they were not willing to stoop to. No principles to guide them. That made them no better than the demons, only weaker.

CHAPTER 9

That night, when the thralls were crawling into their groups and settling down, Dien stared into the night sky. Two moons shone bright in the sky, the Blood Moon shining red down upon them all, and the Bone Moon with its almost bronze light. Even the stars were visible beyond the thin drifts of grey cloud.

Dien tried to remember the last time all three moons had risen on the same night, the last time they had heard Tarkum Chaim's bone chariot rattling across the sky. It was said even the demons feared the Soul Reaver, and every creature small and large knew to hide when the three moons rose together. She wondered if that was a way they could escape, to draw the attention of the Soul Reaver the next time he rode the sky. Another foolish fancy. Everyone knew Tarkum Chaim left none alive, his casket was ever hungry for more souls to steal and serve him. Some fates were far worse even than thralldom.

Helena looked wretched. Too tired to talk, too sad to cry. It broke Dien's heart to see her friend so melancholic. She refused to let Helena succumb, waste away to nothing but a beast of burden like many of the other thralls. She had to pull her back somehow, remind her who she was.

Dien wedged herself in beside Helena, shoulder to shoulder. She was so much taller than the smaller woman now, and broader too. On the other side of Helena, Luci shuffled up against her.

"Urghn," Helena groaned. "This smells like a trap. I'm too tired."

"Wash day tomorrow," Dien said. "I'm surprised you can smell anything."

Helena shot her a pained look. "You are more like your da every day, Dien Hostain. What do you want? I just want to sleep."

"Do you remember old Wormroot?"

Helena's face contorted into an incredulous frown. "The tree?"

"Yes." Dien smiled as she remembered it. "A giant standing proud in the middle of the forest."

Helena shook her head. "I know. I was the first one who took you to see him."

Dien barrelled on. "Taller than any other tree around it and with broad leaves. My ma said he was ancient before the first saplings started to grow around him. We used to hide bone charms inside his little hollows and call them offerings to the old man of the woods."

Helena let slip a pained smile. "I remember. Mostly I remember falling out of the damned tree and bashing my elbow. You dared me to climb all the way to the top and see if I could reach the Caped Moon."

"Well, you were boasting it was possible," Dien said. "If I recall, you barely made the second branch."

"Which was a whole branch higher than you managed." Helena glanced at Dien then and tilted her head to look up at her. "By the Moons and Sun you were actually shorter than me back then. You kept complaining about not being able to find a foothold."

"You both shrieked when you fell," Luci said.

Helena scoffed. "At least we tried. You scampered about below fretting and saying we'd hurt ourselves over and over."

Luci nodded sagely. "Which you did."

Helena made an outraged noise in her throat. "How dare you, Luci Yolk! Weren't hurt at all. I barely had a scratch."

"You cried like Intar's newborn when I rubbed bellflower sap on that scratch," Luci said with a grin.

"Well, you shouldn't have tried to poison me with your hedgewitch nonsense." Helena laughed and the sound was a balm to Dien. It had been so long since they all smiled and laughed together, she had missed it so.

"We nestled in between two big roots, watching the sunset, scraped knees and all," Dien said. "And then the Blood Moon rose to join the Caped."

"I remember," Helena said with a snort. "My parents roused half the village searching for us. My father even lit torches against the Adjudicator's orders. Seems silly now, doesn't it?" She frowned again, and the joy leeched out of her.

"Why are you bringing that up now, Dien? Why remind us of all we've lost?"

"It's not lost, Helena. Wormroot is still there."

"How do you know? How do you know the demons didn't burn the whole forest to the ground along with our village? Everyone we knew is either dead or caged here with us until we die. For all we know, the demons have taken everyone from the Burning Lands to the Ice Plains. There's nothing left, Dien. They've taken everything." She was gripping her fur blanket hard, knuckles white.

Dien tried to think of a way to lift her friends' spirits again. She couldn't let it end on such a sad note.

"Wormroot can't have burned," Luci whispered. "He's too stubborn."

"That's right!" Dien said, leaping on the chance. "Do you know what makes old Wormroot special, Helena?"

Helena pouted at her, then she sighed and her face softened. "Tell me. Please."

"Well, you must have noticed he's different from every other tree in the forest. He's squat while the others grow thin. His leaves are broad instead of needly. He stands alone in the centre of the forest and not another tree grows near. Do you know why?"

Helena shook her head.

"I do," Luci said. "He's not meant to be there. It's too cold for him. My mother says the ground is too hard for trees of his kind, the air is too chilly, and the suns not strong enough."

"But he's too stubborn to quit," Dien said, picking it up. "The embodiment of Berrywhistle and all its people."

Helena rolled her head to the side and raised an eyebrow at Dien. "You have your da's subtlety as well as his humour, Dien Hostain."

Dien ignored her. "He keeps growing even when all the other trees say he shouldn't. Old Wormroot is a wonder, and I bet he's not the only one. There has to be wonders all over the world. I bet... I bet there's a big rock shaped like a rabbit in Black Crag... Or something."

Helena sighed and shook her head. "A rabbit rock?"

Dien shrugged. "Or something?"

"You're not wrong," Gartlen said from the other cage. He was shoved against the bars, and he turned to face them, his blue eyes sparkled in the red light of the Blood Moon. "In the Burning Lands, about two days north of where I was born, there's the Immolate Arch."

Karta stirred and aimed a lazy kick at him. "Shut up, Gartlen. There's no such thing."

"There is, too. It's an arch of flame that shoots out of the earth a hundred paces wide, then crashes back down again. It never stops nor goes out." He smiled and Dien thought he looked handsome, despite the myriad scars crisscrossing his cheeks and nose.

"We used to make a game of it. Fire drips from the arch and we used to run through. If you could cross without singing your arse, you'd have good luck for a full week, we'd say. I kissed my wife for the first time under the Immolate Arch." He chuckled. "Then her hair caught fire."

"You're lying," Karta said.

"Am not."

"You have a wife?" Dien asked.

Gartlen nodded. "Eredae. It means homeless, in her tongue, or so she told me. Wandered down from the Ashlands one day, all on her own. Said her family was gone and she was alone. She was as beautiful as a sunrise and had a temper as dangerous and unpredictable as a black fire roaring from the earth without warning." He grinned. "She took a liking to me, and who wouldn't? I never stood a chance. She gave me two boys before we fled. Erlen and Daelet."

"Where are they?" Dien asked.

Gartlen was silent a moment too long, and the smile that erupted onto his lips seemed forced. "They're free."

"Free?" Karta asked.

Gartlen nodded. "Free." His smile faded.

"There's a shipwreck down near Rivern," Samir said into the silence. "Or where Rivern used to be, I guess. The wreck is so big I can't see how it got there, but folk said it must have sailed up the rivers all the way from the sea. No human ever built a boat so large though. Makes you wonder where it came from, hmm? How it sailed up the rivers and why?"

Karta snorted. "Don't you inlanders keep your histories? Ship that big came from the Exodus. Had to."

"The Exodus?" Dien said.

"Yeah." Karta pulled back her furs and bared one of her arms, the markings tracing a swirling passage down her skin were dark in the moonlight, but as Dien peered through the bars, one of the inkings Karta rubbed at seemed to come alive under her skin. It was a boat with sails up. Her markings stopped just below the boat, and there was nothing below her elbow.

"What's the Exodus?" Dien asked.

Karta pulled her furs over her arms again and sulked, wriggling down until most of her face was covered.

Gartlen grinned and gave her a light shove. "You don't know, do you?"

Karta glared at him. "I know bits. Not supposed to tell it, though. Not without the markings. Didn't get to finish my Lorekeeper schooling before them bloody demons grabbed me."

"Tell us what you do know," Helena said, sounding eager.

"Not supposed to," Karta said. "If I tell it to you inlanders before my markings are complete, I'll never be able to go back to the ice. The Lords

Beneath the Ice will know and they'll break through and swallow me." She rubbed at her face and one of the markings on her cheek came alive: a winged creature with a wide tail and a horn on its head, ice cracking before it.

"You're always saying we're never getting out of these cages," Gartlen said. "So you'll never be going back to the ice anyway. And besides, you hate the cold. Bloody strange thing for an ice walker to hate, but there you are."

"Is it warm in the Burning Lands?" Karta asked.

"Very!" Gartlen said. "Especially if you get caught in a black fire eruption. Now stop changing the subject."

They all waited, eager to hear Karta's story.

"Fine." She bared her arm again and rubbed at the boat marking. It came alive, the wind billowing the sails, the water moving below it. "I don't know much. I only get told the history as I got my markings, and I don't think I'll be getting no more.

"We don't come from here, or at least not all of us did. We fled something. Hundreds and hundreds of years ago, we lived across the sea. The Exodus was when we built hundreds of ships and crossed the angry ocean. Most were lost." She rubbed at another marking, a ship with its hull cracking. The ink came alive and the ship split in two, sinking into the waves. "Some of us came here, settled on the land and on the ice. Never the mountains."

Again, Karta pulled her furs back down over her arm and wriggled into the mound of blankets. "That's all I know. And now I can never go back on the ice, so I hope you're all happy."

"What's the ocean like?" Helena asked.

"Big, cold, and wet," Gartlen said with a chuckle.

"Beautiful," Karta said, her voice wistful. "Endless. Angry and callous and bountiful. We used to make a trek to the west every year, to where the ice ends and the ocean begins." She shook her head, opened her mouth to say more, then closed it again and pulled the furs over her head.

"I think I'd like to go on a boat one day," Helena said. "Not sure about the ice, but I'd like to see the ocean, at least."

Dien could understand that. In Berrywhistle, they'd never seen anything greater than a stream babbling along at a leisurely pace. She couldn't even imagine what the ocean must look like. But far more importantly to Dien, Helena was dreaming again. Imagining being free, exploring the world and seeing its wonders.

CHAPTER 10

Dien heaved on the bellows, dragging down the paddle, her arms, shoulders, and back bunching, straining, popping. Karta, Helena, and Luci had all been dragged to the caves by Roka that morning so the smith had chosen Dien, Enna Rusk, and two women from the farthest cage. Dien didn't know the names of either of the other women, but the sour faced grump beside her was only putting in half the effort and that forced Dien to work all the harder.

"Put your shoulders into it," Dien snapped at the woman.

The woman spat on her feet. "I got toenails older than you, girl."

Dien gritted her teeth as the bellows reached full inflation, and she heaved down on the paddle, blowing air into the forge. It felt like the other woman was barely helping.

Enna Rusk glared at her grumpy companion as sweat poured down her face. "You pull your weight, Narcy, or we'll all be for it."

The next pull was a little easier, the grumpy woman spitting curses as she pulled on the paddle properly for the first time all day.

They were all panting and tired by the time the smith called for a stop. He was making a sword, a jagged strip of iron bathed in blood so many times the metal had turned black. He kept hammering little symbols into the blade, but Dien couldn't figure out the meaning. She often crept to the doorway to peer into the forge whenever they took a break, and always her gaze was drawn to her da's hammer, gathering dust in the corner.

The smith lumbered into the back, already chewing on a steak Dien thought was probably deer. There were none left in the valley, but just yesterday a couple of demons had returned to camp with three large bucks strung up on a pole between them. The smith dumped a cloth packet on the sandy ground. He always fed his workers at mid sun, and it was almost always with meat. One of the few times any of the villagers got to eat real meat, and that made the job a highly sought after one. Many of the men were jealous, but the smith only ever picked women to work the bellows.

Enna Rusk was first to the packet and snatched up the largest steak. Her partner was next and then grumpy woman, Narcy, grabbed both her own piece and the final bit, too. Dien launched forward and grabbed Narcy's wrist, holding her tight. Narcy tried to pull away, but Dien held tight.

"Ow!" Narcy whined. "You're hurting me. Get off me!"

She dropped the final steak into the sand. Dien held her a moment longer, glaring until the smaller woman looked away. Then Dien let her go and she backed away, rubbing at her wrist. Dien stooped and retrieved her meal, brushed off as much sand as she could and then tore off a chunk of meat with her teeth and set to chewing. The smith watched the whole time, a slack expression on his face. Of all the demons, he seemed the most humane. He was still a monster, working the thralls hard, burning them if they slacked. But he also fed them every day and didn't threaten them for meeting his gaze or talking amongst themselves.

"Why the blood?" Dien asked.

"Dien Hostain, you stop it. Stop it right now, you little trouble-making snot!" Enna hissed.

Dien didn't bother pointing out that these days Enna was both shorter and smaller than her. She ignored the older woman and asked the demon again. "Why do you quench the weapons in blood?"

The smith frowned at her, his wide jaw working back and forth. When he spoke, it was slowly. "Blood power. Work runes. Take strong. Make strong. Killing metal."

"Killing who?" Dien said. "Who are you fighting?"

"Flying wings." He grunted. "No talk. Resting now. Work soon."

Dien decided to push her luck. The smith didn't beat her for talking to him, and she was determined to see if she could squeeze some answers from him before he became dangerous.

"Do you have a name? What do the others call you?"

The smith sighed and raised a big hand to scratch at a horn on the bridge of his nose. The skin around it was scarred and tough. Dien realised he did not have many horns, yet he did not seem young to her.

"Brandere," he said and patted a hand against his chest.

Dien patted her own chest. "Dien."

Brandere shrugged, seeming not to care if she had a name or not.

"Is she making friends with it?" Narcy whispered.

"Demon friend," said the other woman. "Just like her da."

Dien ignored them and focused on the smith instead. She wondered if she could get any useful information from him.

"Where do you come from, Brandere?"

"Come from. Land here. Always here."

"But you weren't. Everyone says there was a time when demons were scarce."

The smith growled. Dien quickly took a step back, tried to think of a better way to ask the question. She chewed on a bit of deer and the smith watched her all the while.

"You have to talk stupid like them if you want them to understand," Enna said sullenly. "Before land. Before here. Where before?"

Brandere grunted and narrowed his eyes. "Before below."

"See," Enna said. "You just have to talk stupid."

"I guess you get a lot of practice," Dien said.

Enna sneered at her. "Fine. Don't thank me for the help, you ignorant scab."

"Sorry. I didn't mean..."

"Yes you did."

Dien drew in a deep breath and let it out slowly. Her ma had once told her, Enna Rusk was how she was to protect herself. No one in the village liked to talk about it, but she hadn't lived an easy life. Her father had beaten her often for any perceived slight or mistake, and every adult in the village had known and done nothing about it. Enna had learned to tend to her own wounds, care for herself, avoid others, most of all her own father. Then her father had died from a wound gone bad after cutting himself with a skinning knife. A tragedy, so everyone said, the talk of the village for weeks, and no one mentioned the pain he'd visited on his own daughter.

It didn't end there for Enna. She'd married a young woodsman by the name of Kork Rusk. Three years on and no children, and Kork was regularly at the village tavern blaming his barren wife. Dien heard her own da speak of it from time to time, thinking his voice didn't carry between the walls of their hut. But Dien knew if she pressed her ear against the wooden wall, she could hear the soft murmur of his voice. He said it wasn't right that Kork spoke of such things for all the village to hear. But again no one stopped Kork from speaking, and because of that the whole village thought it was Enna's fault they'd had no children.

Dien had never liked Enna. The older woman always seemed so cold and angry, and was forever spreading rumours about Dien, calling her mad, a wastrel, a harlot. She'd never been able to understand why Enna had made up such lies, nor why she was always targeting her. She wondered if maybe it was her way of coping with the life she'd lived, passing on the pain to another. It wasn't right. But that didn't mean she deserved whatever she got.

"Thank you, Enna," Dien said. She gave the older woman a respectful nod.

Enna frowned at her, then snorted and turned away, gnawing on the fatty gristle of her steak in private.

Dien turned back to the smith. The demon was watching them in silence, dark eyes flicking between them. "Before now. Before below. Before this you were below, um, underground?"

The smith scratched at the tough skin around his nose horn again. "Before below. Big then. Many big. Now above." He shook his head. "Better below."

"Better below? Why?" Dien pressed. "Why was it better below?"

"Hotter before. More heat. No fight. No wings. Flying now. Fight now. Better below."

It was a confusing jumble of statements Dien didn't understand. The wings and the flying and the fighting all seemed to be something the smith thought they were dealing with. Yet Dien had seen no fighting. No demons with wings.

"You were underground," she said. "Before below. There was no fighting. No fight. Why did you leave? Why come above ground? Um. Now here. Why here?"

The smith chewed on the last bit of deer steak, swallowed. "Dark come. Living dark. Many hands. Hunt mothers. Kill many. Run then. Land now. Above now." The demon smiled at her. "Meat here. Weak meat. Working meat. Better below."

The smith stopped and stood suddenly, growling and rolling his head. "Working meat. Pump now. More heat. Working meat."

The demon reached out casually and gave Dien a push. She stumbled back, fell awkwardly against the bellows. "Pump now," the smith said as he stalked to the other side of the forge.

Dien shoved the last of her deer steak into her mouth and started chewing even as she climbed onto the paddle and waited for the others to join her.

"Good work," said Narcy. "Thanks for cutting short our break, Hostain."

"More heat!" the smith roared from the other side of the forge.

All four of them heaved down on the paddles to get the bellows pumping. Dien struggled to breathe past the steak she still hadn't swallowed. Opposite her, Enna Rusk watched through narrowed eyes, saying nothing.

CHAPTER 11

THE WEEKS SLOUCHED ON. DIEN NEVER FORGOT HER HOPES, the beginnings of her plan to escape, but she also didn't share it with anyone else. She wasn't yet sure who she could trust. And she still had no way to escape the hounds that would be sent to track them once they ran.</p>

She thought she could probably trust Karta and Samir, they seemed stout sorts. She was less certain about Gartlen. He was loud and obnoxious, but there was something solid about him that Dien couldn't quite reason out. She wanted to trust him, she just wasn't sure she could.

Helena and Luci were beyond question, but Dien didn't want to burden them with the secret before it was time.

Helena's mood soured again and she seemed to grow more fragile by the day, as though the will to live was leaking out of her like a water skin with a hole in it. She ate, slept, worked, but there was no longer any trace of the vibrant young woman who had talked the days away in Berry-whistle and who had dreamed of adventure. Dien mourned that loss even while her friend still lived and desperately wanted to find a way to bring her back.

After Metwit's death, Donnel only became a worse bully. As they were marched back to the cages after a day's work, he sometimes made a grab for other thralls, tried to force them into the cage with him and his cronies. One day he managed to grab an older thrall by the name of Tentry. The demons didn't care. Dien woke in the middle of the deep night to hear muffled cries and thumps. In the morning, Tentry was dead.

Donnel merely shrugged. "Must have died in his sleep, the poor sod. Old men do that, everyone knows it's true."

The demons dragged the body away and that night there was meat in the broth. Donnel and his friends laughed, and Dien thought that had been the point all along. There were fewer and fewer deer in the forest and meat was getting scarcer in the valley. The thralls mostly ate mushrooms and berries. Donnel was not happy with that, and he was willing to kill to get some meat.

It disgusted Dien. She pushed the bowl away as soon as it was handed to her. Helena stared into the broth a few moments, then looked at Dien and shrugged. She curled into a ball and shivered.

Luci paused with the bowl against her lips. She had a pained look on her face like she really couldn't decide what to do. Dien said nothing. She would not try to impose her principles on anyone else. Eventually Luci lowered the bowl and pushed it away. Enna Rusk snorted and grabbed it, slurping greedily and handing Helena's untouched bowl to Panyet.

Dien realised Samir's bowl was at his feet, also untouched. He was staring at her, scratching at his beard.

"It takes a person of rare courage to stand when everyone else kneels. And it takes a person of ever rarer heart to inspire others to stand with them." The old trader glanced down at the bowl again, then up at Dien. He tipped the bowl over with his foot.

Karta sighed from the next cage over. "Frost take you bloody people, you'll be the death of me." She handed her bowl to Gartlen. Gartlen merely shrugged and started eating.

Dien's pick struck the wall and a chip of stone flew off and smacked her in the face. She winced and let the pick go, which stuck in the wall of the mine, and touched her face where the stone had hit her. In the grimy, flickering light of the torch, she could see blood on her fingertips.

"Let me see," Gartlen said. He laid his own pick down and grabbed the torch, holding it close enough to her face she could feel the heat of it. He stared at the wound and Dien stared at him. He had eyes as blue as a deep lake. "Yep. That's a good one. Hope you like scars."

Dien shrugged and wrenched her pick from the wall. "Some days I think we're nothing but scars."

Gartlen coughed. "Sorry. The maudlin was so thick I choked on it."

Dien shot him a baleful stare, but she couldn't hold it in the face of his wide grin. Soon she was smiling too. "I suppose I was overdoing it a little."

Gartlen nodded. "I thought I was here with Helena for a moment."

"She used to be the life and soul of Berrywhistle," Dien said. "You couldn't help but smile when she was around."

"This place will do that to ya. Soul crushing, as my granddaddy used to say it. Fire bless him. He was crushed. Tried milking a cow and didn't realise he had a bull."

"How do you manage it?" Dien asked, leaning against the wall. It was oddly quite warm against her back. "You've been here longer than anyone and you don't seem crushed."

Gartlen put the torch back in the brazier and leaned next to her, grinning through his patchy red beard. "Ahh, but there's my trick. I never had a soul to crush." He winked at her.

"No stop!" Roka roared as he stalked into the little cavern. "Work meat. Swinging pick. Dig now. No stop."

Dien and Gartlen moved as one, pushing away from the wall and grabbing their picks. Before she could swing it, she felt the sting of the demon's whip lash across her back. A grunt from Gartlen said he'd received the same. She didn't let the pain stop her; it would only drive Roka to greater punishment. She hit the wall with the pick and drew back for another strike. Beside her, Gartlen did the same.

Roka stalked back and forth behind them for a while. They worked in silence, a steady staccato of metal striking stone. Echoing footsteps announced Samir's arrival, carrying buckets. They took it in turns during the day; two people with the picks, scraping away at the cave wall, one person filling the buckets with rocks and stone chips, then carting them outside. A fat demon with a drooping eye waited outside. He sorted the rocks, deciding which were useless, which contained metal ore, and which were the rocks that burned.

Samir gathered rocks from the ground in silence, and Roka shoved him aside and stormed away. He had four other teams to terrorise down different corridors. As soon as the demon was out of sight, Gartlen eased up and went back to leaning against the wall. Dien kept swinging her pick against the wall, but she didn't put in half as much effort as before. As long as Roka heard them working, he would be less likely to come back.

"I've been calculating the days and weeks," Samir said as he rummaged around on the ground and plucked a fist sized rock into the bucket. "It's been almost a year since your village was attacked. Almost a year as thralls to these bastards."

Dien's next swing had no force behind it. The pick bounced off the stone without so much as chipping free a pebble. A whole year of toil, of fearing for her life, for the lives of her friends. A year since everything she had known was torn away.

"Only a year?" Gartlen asked. "They pass so quick. I think I was close to Dien's age when they got me. Now I'm..." He threw up his arms in an expansive shrug. "Older?"

Dien glanced at him and smiled. "Definitely old."

"I'll have you know silver hair is a mark of distinction in the Burning Lands. Marked me out from among my friends. Eredae used to say it made me look like lightning against the night sky."

Dien drew back her pick and struck the wall again, putting some real effort behind it this time. Had it really been a year since her parents were murdered?

"Do you know about my da?" she asked. It was a question that had been gnawing at her for so long now, but she'd never had the courage to ask it before. Everyone seemed to have heard the name Hostain, but no one had told her why.

A pointed silence erupted in the small cavern and Dien turned to find Gartlen and Samir staring at each other. "You do know," she said. "Tell me. Why did Donnel call him the Peace Breaker? Why did he kill my da?"

Samir gave up hunting the floor for stones and sat. "Things weren't always this bad," he said. "Just twenty years ago, demon attacks were fewer and not as brutal. We still lost a village here and there, maybe two a year, but mostly the demons just led raids. Took a few people. We had forges, fires. I remember sitting round a campfire as a kid, singing along to some old tune Jolen played on his lute. What was his favourite? *The Ballad of Black Barni*, that was it. Merrier tune, I never heard, even if Jolen couldn't hold a note." He sighed. "Fire and music and no fear it'd bring the demons down on us. Well, almost no fear.

"The villages did fight amongst each other, though. Every now and then there'd be a raid, some people would die. The losers would give what they could to send the victors away. But there was always the threat of demons. So the Adjudicators set up a Folkmoot, the biggest there'd ever been. From the Ice Plains to the Ashlands. Mountain folk, river folk, forest folk. Hundreds of villages sent their Adjudicators to talk in peace and discuss what to do about the demons. There was even talk of... heh... fighting back.

"The peace held for three days while talks went on. Then a young man by the name of Unter Hostain broke it. Your da was bodyguard to his Adjudicator, some village to the east, I think, can't remember the name. Your da killed an Adjudicator from another village. Broke the peace and ran."

"Why?" Dien asked.

"For love," Gartlen said dramatically with a flourish. Then he shrugged. "Or for revenge. Or some people just said he was mad. No one ever seemed to be able to decide why he did it. I think love makes for the most thrilling of versions though. He did it for his lady love, whose hand he was denied." He clutched a hand to his heart. "So romantic."

Samir shook his head. "In the end, the why isn't important. It was done. Your da killed an Adjudicator and fled. Peace was broken and the Folkmoot went from talking to bloody battle in the space of a day."

Gartlen sighed. "The line between peace and violence is thin and brittle."

Samir nodded. "Lots of people died. And then the demons attacked. They came in numbers we'd not realised existed before. Hundreds of demons just poured into the Folkmoot and... well, you know full well what they do by now, Dien. I don't think they were quite so organised back then. People escaped, fled to their villages, warned their people. And they spread word what your da had done. Peace Breaker, they called him."

"Demon friend," Gartlen said.

Dien looked at him so sharply, Gartlen held up his hands. "Mercy."

"My da was no friend to any demon," she hissed at him.

Gartlen snorted. "Well, that hardly matters. It's what people said. For a long time it was dangerous just to say the name Hostain. Everyone thought it would bring the demons to your village as sure as lighting a great bloody fire."

Dien still had her pick in hand. Her blood was thumping through her veins, making her hot like it was on fire. She leaned against the pick, scraped it down the wall, tearing loose little flakes of rock to crash to the ground at her feet.

She couldn't understand it. Her da had always been kind, gentle. He'd never hurt anyone. He had the strength to, there was no doubting that, but he never used it for violence. Even when Donnel and his cronies had attacked, her father had taken the beating. He hadn't fought back. Why wouldn't he have fought back if he could have? Why hadn't he caved in Donnel's head then and there? He'd still be alive if he had. He might have fought for them, won them free. They might all be free if he had just stood his ground and fought back instead of cowering while smaller men hit him for petty vengeance.

Dien reared back and swung her pick at the wall as hard as she could. She shouted and struck again and again and again, each time knocking free a chunk of rock. She couldn't decide who she hated more; Donnel for killing her father, or her father for letting it happen, for not being the man he could have been and protecting his family.

She struck the wall again, snarling at it, tears streaming down her face.

"Dien..." It was Gartlen, saying her name. She realised it wasn't the first time. He held out a hand. "Dien, stop." He grabbed hold of her pick on the backswing, held it firm. "I'm sorry. I didn't mean to say your da was—"

"QUIET MEAT!" Roka roared from behind as he thundered towards them.

Gartlen grunted and let go of her pick as Roka's whip lashed him across the arm. He fell back against the wall, cradling his arm against his chest. The demon closed on him, ignoring Samir picking up rocks on the floor and Dien, her pick raised and all but forgotten in her hands.

"No talking. Working meat. Quiet meat. Work now." The demon advanced on Gartlen, shoving him back against the wall, snarling in his face.

Gartlen lowered his head, stooped, stared at the rocky ground. He said nothing, only cradled his arm. Roka pushed him against the wall hard, shoved his face against the rock until Gartlen whined in pain.

"Listen meat. No talking. Working meat. Listen meat." Roka kept Gartlen's head pushed against the wall and reached up with his other hand. His claws closed around Gartlen's ear and with a sick tearing sound he ripped the flesh away.

Gartlen fell to his knees, clutching at his head, mewling in pain. Roka held up his severed prize, grinning at it. "Listening meat." The demon laughed.

Dien's blood was on fire now. She raised her pick to drive it deep into Roka's back. Gartlen lurched forwards, shoved Dien and knocked her back. She staggered, her strike going wide and hitting the wall in a shower of sparks. Roka turned back to them, still holding Gartlen's ear. His bug eyes were wide and furious.

Gartlen snatched up his own pick and slammed it against the wall. He kept his eyes down. "Working meat," he said, his voice tight with pain. Blood ran down his face. "We're working. See."

Roka waved the severed ear about. "Listen meat." He held the ear close to his mouth. "Listen meat." He turned and walked away, laughing to himself. "Listen meat."

Gartlen stared cold fury after the demon until he was devoured by the darkness. Then he sagged and fell to his knees. "Quiet quiet. Listen meat," he said, his voice as full as scorn as pain. "Fire burn you, you piece of shit. I'll talk. I'll sing the bloody song of your demise." He winced and grit his teeth, groaning. "Shit, this hurts."

"We best wrap that," Samir said. He was already picking at the stitching of his sleeve to pull the fur away. "Dien, keep up on that wall while I tie this around his head. Best we can do is put pressure on it. It's a bad wound, but it should stop bleeding eventually."

"Wonderful," Gartlen sneered.

Dien swung her pick at the wall. "You do hate them," she said. She'd been wondering if she could really trust Gartlen. Now she thought she had her answer.

Gartlen laughed incredulously. "Fire's Light, Dien, of course I hate them. Every damned one of them."

"Sorry." She hit the wall again, a rock tumbled loose. "It's just that most of the time you seem almost content here."

He stared up at her with a disgusted look that broke into a wincing curse as Samir wrapped the fur around his head and pressed it tight over the wound.

"Content?" Gartlen choked out a laugh. "Try morbidly resigned. You know, I'm from the Burning Lands. You might have had it easy for a while, but we never have. The demons take and take and take. I couldn't handle it anymore. Didn't want it for my boys. When I fled west, there were eight of us. My wife, two sons. Four others from another family." He snorted. "I can't even remember their faces."

"The other family?"

Gartlen choked on a sob. "Them either. I can't remember their names but I remember what they tas..." He stopped, sat down and pushed Samir away roughly. "I have been here *so long*."

Dien hit the wall once more and let the pick fall from her hands to clatter against the ground. She sank to her knees next to Gartlen. "It's alright," she said, placing a hand on his shoulder. He recoiled.

"Shut up!" Gartlen snapped. "What do you know of alright, you stupid..."

"That's enough!" Samir snapped. He stood, towered over them both, seeming menacing in the flickering torch light.

Gartlen lowered his head and took a deep breath, let it out as a stuttering sigh. Dien watched him force his frustration down. Then he smiled and seemed completely recovered, his normal jovial air returned.

"What about you, Dien Hostain, daughter of a traitor? Don't you hate our gracious captors?"

"With all my heart. With every drop of my will and every bit of strength in my blood."

Gartlen paused, staring at her with his mouth hanging open. "Bit dramatic, but what else should I expected from you? Is that why you whisper to Helena every night about how you're going to escape?"

Dien stood slowly and hefted her pick. She drew back and slammed it against the wall. "Helena is dying in here. Day by day more of her is worn away. They did that to her. They robbed my friend of her joy. That is what they do. They take away everything that makes us human. Scrape us out and make us hollow so we don't resist, don't fight back, don't do anything but work and obey. They would make beasts of us."

Dien drew back and hit the wall as hard as she could with the pick. A chunk of stone as large as her head fell away to crumble on the ground. "I whisper to Helena every night because I will not allow her to give up. I won't let them kill her, nor scrape her out into a hollow shell. We're not beasts. We're human. I'm going to get out of here and I'm going to..."

"Quiet!" Gartlen hissed. He held up a hand and the frown on his face said he was serious.

Dien was panting from the effort of striking the wall. She lowered her pick and listened as Gartlen closed on the wall, his head cocked to the side so his remaining ear was almost pressed against the rock.

Dien stilled her heaving breath and heard a deep, low, rasping inhalation.

Gartlen shook his head wildly and backed away from the wall. "Oh, Fire! We need to go. Now."

"Why?" Dien asked. "What is it?" She realised there was a dark hole in the wall where her pick had struck and knocked a chunk of rock away was a black abyss. They'd accidentally tunnelled into another cave,

Gartlen looked like he was caught between explaining and running away in a blind panic. He shook his head and winced at the pain in his ear, then gestured towards Samir. "Torch," he whispered. "Bring me the torch."

Samir stood and grabbed the torch, handing it over. Gartlen held it up so the flickering light shone into the darkness beyond. They crept closer, peering through the hole. Something moved on the other side, a great mound of scaly darkness shifting, rising and falling. Dien couldn't see it clearly, but it was massive, and it appeared to be slumbering in the cave on the other side of the wall. She remembered the man on the journey to Demonholme, running into a cave, the screams of terror and pain as he died to some unknown monstrosity. The demons laughing and moving everyone on. Was this what he had run into?

Gartlen backed away from the wall, taking the torch with him. Dien and Samir followed. Once they were a few paces away, Gartlen sighed. "There are things in these mountains that even the demons fear. Things even the big demons don't disturb. We tell Roka what we found. The demons will close down this mine. Better for everyone." He started away.

Dien grabbed Gartlen's arm. This was the opportunity she'd been waiting for. A way out. "What if we don't?" she whispered, glancing around to make sure Roka wasn't nearby. "What if we work on another wall, pretend we never found anything."

"Why?" Gartlen asked.

Samir smiled. "You have a plan?"
Dien nodded. "A way to get us out of here."

CHAPTER 12

That night Dien waited until everyone had fallen asleep. Helena and Luci were curled up together, buried beneath a mound of furs. Karta was leaning against the wall of her own cage, snoring like a grinding mill. Dien listened to Enna and Panyet humping in the darkness, then waited until after they had stopped, long after Enna's quiet sobs faded. Even the murmur and laughter from Donnel's cage eventually fell silent. Still, she waited in the dark. The Caped Moon shone down on them sullenly, giving the darkness an ethereal blue haze.

Only once she was certain everyone was asleep did she kick Samir in the arm to wake him. He roused with a groan and sat up quietly. Gartlen was still awake, leaning against the bars, she could see his eyes shining in the blue light. He nodded in silence and shook Karta. She snapped awake and grabbed his throat, but he eased her hand away and they both crept closer to the bars. Lastly, Dien shook Helena and Luci awake, leaning close and pressing her hand to their lips, warning them to be quiet. They gathered around the bars between their cage and Gartlen's, pressed close together and whispering in voices so quiet even Dien herself struggled to hear them.

"I've been searching for a way out," Dien said. "A way to get us all free. I think, I've found it."

Karta snorted. "You woke me up for this? I've no wish to see my own innards."

"Quiet," Gartlen said. "She's serious."

"What? You, too? Gartlen, you've been in here too long to listen to this shit. Remember Jess? I haven't forgotten. There is no way out."

"Just shut up, Karta. Listen to her." Gartlen nodded in the darkness. "Tell them."

"I'm in," Helena said a bit too loudly.

Dien smiled at her. "You haven't even heard..."

"I don't care. I don't care, I don't care, I don't care!" She sobbed. "I can't take it in here, Dien. I want out. I don't care if I die anymore. I just want to be free. I want freedom." She was crying, fat tears rolling down her cheeks and dripping from her chin. Dien had known she was struggling, but she hadn't realised just how close to breaking Helena was. "If you have a way out. I'm in. Just get me out of here."

"Escape?" Enna Rusk said a little too loudly in the dark. Noise carried far too well at night and some of the demons never slept. Even now Dien could hear them around their fires, laughing and shouting.

Enna appeared from the gloom, crawling from the other side of the cage. Her face was twisted into a nasty sneer. "You silly little girl! There is no escape. None of us are ever getting out of here. There's no hope."

Dien thought she saw something else, hidden below Enna's scorn: desperation. She looked at the others, those she had grown up with and those she had come to consider friends. Samir slumped, beaten before their plan was even shared. Karta nodded and placed her back against the stone wall, closed her eyes. Gartlen rested his head against the bars. Even Luci looked broken by Enna's words. She curled in on herself, twisting her hands together into knots. It had taken so little to break them. Even before she had shared her plan, just a few harsh words had reminded them all how little chance they had. How hope had forsaken this place, and all of them along with it.

Helena reached out and gripped Dien's hands. She had stopped crying and there was something new in her face now. Not the grim acceptance of the others, nor the weary resignation. There was a fierce determination in the set of her jaw. Dien saw her friend again for the first time in so long. Not the husk she had become, long since given up and waiting to die; but the young woman who dreamed of freedom and adventure.

Helena gave Dien's hands a squeeze and nodded.

"Hope?" Dien said, staring into Helena's eyes. She saw it there, and it was not yet vanished. "You say it is lost, Enna." She looked at the older woman, crouching at the edge of their group. "You're wrong. There is always hope as long as you have the courage to hold on to it. It's the one thing they can never take from us."

Dien glanced at the others, meeting each of their gazes in turn. "They can maim us, kill us, bury us in humiliation. They can force us to work their forges, dig their mines, gather their food. But I still hope for escape or rescue. For freedom." She chuckled. "Even for the chance to repay them for every moment of suffering they have heaped upon me. I hope.

"They cannot take that away from me, from us. Not as long as we hold on to it in our hearts. Not unless we give it to them. And I refuse to give these bastards anything. So I still have hope. I will not give them my hope. And I beg you, please don't give up. Hold on to it. Do not let them break you."

A silence fell. Dien could hear snoring from the next cage over.

Enna Rusk was the first to speak, her voice low and desperate. "You tell me true, Dien Hostain. You tell me true right now. Can you get us out of here?" There was the hope Enna had claimed was lost. It was alive and well. She had not yet let go of it.

"I have a plan." Dien said. She looked to Gartlen. "It will work. Tell them it will work."

Gartlen had his hands wrapped around the bars as if he could throttle them. "It might. If it doesn't get us all killed."

"Don't sound like much of a plan," Enna said.

"What do you care?" Helena snapped at her.

"Shut it, girl. You think I like it here? You think I like opening my legs to that scarred up simpleton every night?"

Helena glared at Enna. "You seem to enjoy it well enough."

"Sun and Moons curse you, Helena Tressel, you stupid girl. You don't know the first thing about it. You didn't lose a husband in the raid. You don't have Donnel Ocha and his slavering thugs pawing at you every night, trying to pull you into their cage. I do what I must to survive, just like you. Just like all of you. Don't you try to sit there pretending you're better than me."

Helena looked away, abashed. "Sorry. I didn't..."

Enna spat on the rocky ground. "Don't need your apologies. Can you really get me out, Dien Hostain?"

"I can."

"It'll work," Samir said in a voice heavy with confidence. Dien thanked him for that. "Or it will get us all killed and we'll be no worse off anyway."

Dien told them all the plan then. It was a simple thing, but Dien remembered one time when she'd been watching her da build a cabinet for Arnut Poll's various herbs and medicines. He'd said *A simple joint might not do as much as a complex one, but there's less to go wrong. Simplicity and functionality over all else.*

The first step of the plan was the easiest. They had to steal some grease from the butcher. Dien took it upon herself. The next time she had to get a new torch, she'd take a bowl with her. The moment the butcher's back was turned, she'd scoop some of the grease and hide it beneath her furs. They didn't need much, just enough to slather over the hinges of the cage doors. They needed to stop the doors from squealing and alerting the demon hounds. Once they did that, they could sneak out in the dead of night when all the other thralls and most of the demons were asleep.

As soon as they were out of the cages, they'd circle the camp back to the cave they'd found earlier. Samir and Gartlen would spend the day working on it, carefully making the hole in the wall large enough for a person to slip through. It was dangerous, with a monster ferocious enough to scare the demons slumbering on the other side, but that danger was also why the plan would work.

They'd squeeze through the hole, sneak past the monster, and flee. The monster had gotten down there somehow, so there had to be a way out. The demons wouldn't follow and without the demon hounds to track them, they would be free just as soon as they worked their way back up to the surface. From there, Karta could lead them west to the edge of the mountains where the great forest stretched on beyond the horizon.

As soon as she'd explained the plan, the others started adding their own contributions. Luci most often worked collecting mushrooms. She could work a little harder and squirrel away an extra basket. It wouldn't be much, but it might keep them going a day or two while they found food somewhere else. Enna worked the forge and said there was always loose strips of leather hanging around. She could steal a strip or two, enough to fashion a crude sling. If they brought down a bird or one of those rock rabbits they could eat well for a night. Karta offered to get some more furs, the demons rarely even bothered her when she went to collect more these days.

Before the first light of sun brightened the sky, they had a plan. But more importantly, they had hope, and the will to enact their escape. And none of them were willing to wait. They all looked up at those first rays of light, and Dien swore it would be their final day in Demonholme.

Dien hadn't felt so enthused in longer than she could remember. Renewed energy pulsed through her veins and every step was a little lighter. She went to the mine with Gartlen and Samir and they worked on a different wall. If Roka noticed that they had switched walls, the demon didn't care. Dien suspected he knew little of the rocks and was only there to ensure the thralls worked. Once Roka was out of sight, they took turns to sneak back to the hole and scrap away at it, slowly making it larger until Dien was certain even Samir could squeeze himself through.

The scaly monster on the other side continued to slumber, its breathing loud and slow, rumbling enough to shake stones free from the wall. Dien shoved the torch through the hole and peered in. Whatever it was, the creature was massive. Dark scales, feet as big as her cabin back in Berrywhistle. She couldn't see its head, but it was so big the torch was a single star trying to light up the whole night sky. Dien wondered if this beast was the thing the demons had fled from. The smith had said *Big come. Many big. Flying wings.* She withdrew from the hole carefully, making as little noise as possible.

She snuffed out the torch with a strip of fur and when Roka ordered her to get a new one, she spirited the old torch away, depositing it in a nook at the cave's mouth.

Dien approached the butchery with a nervousness she couldn't quite suppress. The wooden bowl, so often filled with broth, was wiped clean and hidden under her furs, pressed tight against her stomach. One of the demon hounds was lounging about the butchery and as always it reared its head when she approached. The demon rose slowly, stretched, and followed her. This was where the plan could fail. If she had misjudged the hounds, if they could communicate with the other demons, then the moment she tried to steal the grease, the butcher would know. But this was why she had taken the task for herself. The risk was all hers. If she failed, she'd be strung up, but none of the others would suffer.

"What meat? What want?" the butcher roared at her.

Dien kept her head down as the demon towered over her, so close she could smell the death on it. The demon hound crowded in beside her, a mound of muscle and mangy fur. "New torch," Dien said in a shaky voice. "Roka needs a new torch."

The butcher turned with a dismissive wave. "New torch. Blind meat. Come now."

Dien hurried after the butcher, the hound padding close on her heels. The butcher started shifting barrels, lugging the barrel of grease right in front of her. Dien wormed her hand inside her furs, reached up to where the wooden bowl was cupped against her skin. The demon hound stepped closer, sniffed at her, growled low in its throat. It was now or never. She had to trust the hound was a mindless beast, just like any other dog.

Dien whipped the bowl down and out of her furs, scooped it into the jiggling grease, and then whisked it away, pressing it close against her skin to stop any of the oozing gloop from escaping. Trembling, she turned her head to look at the hound, dread creeping along her spine. The demon watched her, beady red eyes glaring at her like the prey she was. It edged closer, lips pulling back, saliva dropping.

"New torch."

Dien couldn't take her eyes from the demon hound. She was sure it knew what she had done, that it was about to reveal her crime.

"New torch," the butcher shouted and thrust the torch at her. Dien caught it and staggered from the force, barely keeping the bowl of grease pressed against her skin. "Weak meat." The butcher turned away and went back to lugging the barrels under cover.

Dien turned and fled. The demon hound followed her for a way, but eventually turned back towards the butchery. She was right. It hadn't revealed her. No more than a mindless beast. She ran back to the cave and spent the rest of the day collecting the rocks Gartlen and Samir chipped away, always keeping one hand on the bowl of grease pressed against her skin underneath her furs.

That evening, none of them could hide their nervous excitement. The demons led them back to the cages, pulled open the gates with wrenching squeals, shoved them all through, then closed the gates behind them. Dien saw Donnel Ocha try to grab Enna, pull her into their cage, but Panyet shoved the smaller man out of the way and Enna scurried in with them. That was good. Dien didn't want to risk opening Donnel's cage as well, but now Enna was with them she wouldn't leave the woman behind. They were *all* getting out.

Dien hid the bowl of grease at the back of the cage, beneath a mound of furs. All they had to do was wait until night blanketed the world and all the others had drifted off to sleep.

Gartlen paced, oddly nervous. Dien had never seen him so restless.

He kept glancing at the sky as if he couldn't understand why it was still so light.

When the demons came to feed them, Swordere and his hounds stalked along with them. The leader of Demonholme never fed the thralls. Dien felt a knot of fear crush her insides. It grew tighter when she realised none of the demons had brought food. There was something wrong and the timing was too terrible to be a coincidence. She stood, leaving Luci and Helena huddled together, and stepped up next to Samir. The old trader was trembling. He backed against the bars, twisted his hand around the iron, shot Dien a pained look.

Swordere walked along the outside of the cages, trailing a claw across the bars. He had a new horn, jutting out from his chin, the tip just poking through bleeding black and red flesh. The demon hounds followed close on his heels, snarling.

"Running meat," Swordere said as he walked along outside the cages. "Escaping meat."

It was impossible. Dien couldn't see how he had known. They'd done everything quietly. Even if the demon hound had somehow told him she'd stolen the grease, how could he have known she meant to use it to escape?

"NO ESCAPE!" Swordere screamed.

Dien jumped, terrified. Her knees were weak, her legs shaking so badly she almost collapsed.

Swordere wrenched open the gate to their cage with a squeal and took a step inside. "Which meat?"

Dien realised the demon was staring to the other end of the cage, his gaze locked on Enna Rusk. Enna raised a trembling hand and pointed at Dien. "It was her. She's the one planning to escape."

Dien locked her knees but she couldn't stop the shaking. She turned slowly and stared up at Swordere. The demon grinned down at her.

"No escape. Suffer now." Swordere stalked forward. Dien closed her eyes, but the demon shoved her aside. She careened into the bars with a thud, pain erupting in her shoulder. Swordere reached down and grabbed Helena by her hair. Helena screamed, feet kicking against the rocks as the demon dragged her out of the cage.

Dien lurched to her feet and ran after them even as Swordere pushed the gate closed behind him. Helena was still screaming, pleas mixing with pain. Dien hit the gate, pushed against it as hard as she could. It barely shifted, but it squealed with protest. One of the demon hounds pounced, snarling. It smacked against the gate hard enough to send Dien stumbling back. She fell on her arse.

It wasn't right. Wasn't fair.

"Stop it!" Dien screamed at Swordere as he dragged Helena away. "It wasn't her. It was me. I'm the one who tried to escape, not her."

Swordere stopped, turned, stalked back to the cage. He wrenched Helena by her hair, dragged her along.

She was crying, pleading, blood running down from her hair and mixing with her tears. "Let me go. I'm sorry. I'm sorry. I won't run. I'm sorry."

Dien couldn't let Helena suffer in her place.

Swordere stopped by the bars and stared down at her. He wrenched Helena up by her hair, slammed her against the bars, pressing her body against the metal. "Your fault. Pain meat. Example meat. Your fault."

Helena was crying, her face screwed up, tears and blood running. "I'm sorry," she cried.

Dien grabbed Helena's hand, gripped in both of her own as if she could just hold on strongly enough she could stop her from being taken.

"It was me," Dien shouted up at Swordere. "Take me."

The demon held her gaze for a few seconds, then he grinned wide. He turned and stalked away, back to the camp, dragging Helena with him.

Dien howled and ran to the gate again. The demon hounds snapped and snarled, guarding it. She didn't care. She couldn't let it happen. Samir wrapped his arms around her, dragged her back. Dien tried to fight, flinging herself about to get free, but the old trader held on tight, dragged her away and pulled her down. She knelt there, bawling in his arms until she was so tired she couldn't anymore. Samir released her and sat back against the bars, shaking his head.

Then Helena started to scream.

Dien curled her hands into fists and slammed them against the rocky ground. She looked up at Enna Rusk backed up as far away as she could, huddling against the other side of the cage.

"Why?" Dien snarled. She rose unsteadily to her feet and took a step towards the older woman. "Why? Why? Why? Why?" She couldn't think of any other words.

Panyet stood, positioned himself between them.

"Why Enna?" Dien howled. "WHY?"

Panyet lashed out and his fist smashed into Dien's jaw. She collapsed, sprawling on the ground. Samir was up again in a moment, pulling her away and squaring up to Panyet, but the younger man didn't make any other moves.

Dien lay in the middle of the cage, weeping, listening to Helena fill the valley with her pain. There was nothing she could do. Not for Helena. Not against Enna. There was nothing she could do.

Luci crept closer and heaved Dien up. Dien turned and buried her head in Luci's lap, sobbed.

She heard Donnel chuckle. "Wonder if we'll get some proper food tomorrow?" Some of the others in his cage laughed with him.

Helena screamed all night and Dien listened to it all.

CHAPTER 13

THE NEXT MORNING AS THE SUN TURNED THE MOUNTAIN TOPS to molten fire, the demons came to the cages. Over forty of them, one for each of the surviving thralls. Almost half of Demonholme if Dien was any judge of numbers. The thralls were dragged out of their cages far more roughly than was needed and then marched into the camp straight towards the butchery.

Dien hung her head and desperately sought the numbness that she knew she'd need. That same void of feeling that had afflicted her after Berrywhistle. But it eluded her. Even after a night of listening to her most cherished friend scream herself bloody. Even after shedding every tear she could until her eyes dried up. Dien still couldn't feel numb. Instead, she experienced everything more sharply. She felt every stone beneath her calloused feet, every pinch of skin as the demon's claw wrapped around her arm and dragged her on. The sun was glaringly bright. She couldn't block any of it out.

"Don't look," Karta whispered.

"Quiet meat!" The demon dragging Karta gave her a rough shake by the arm.

Dien had forgotten that Karta had been through this herself. When the villagers from Berrywhistle had first arrived, a man had been strung up. Dien had never asked for the full story, but it was clear that Karta and Jess had been friends. Perhaps more than friends. And she had seen him every day, bleeding, dying, in such pain he couldn't even cry out.

Dien felt herself dragged to a stop. She stared at the rocky ground, picked out small rocks, a crawler working its leggy way between them all. It had an iridescent shell. She sniffed and smelled blood.

"Look meat." Roka grabbed her hair and wrenched her head up.

Helena was strung up next to a deer carcass. Her hands were cinched so tightly to the line above her fingers had turned purple and swollen. She was stripped, naked, her belly sliced open and her guts spilling out into a bucket. Dien retched, but there was nothing in her stomach and Roka didn't let go of her hair.

Swordere stalked about in front of Helena, one of his hounds trailing his every step. The other hound sat before Helena like it was just waiting for the chance to feed. Dien hoped Swordere gave the order. A quick death by demon hound was the only mercy she could think of now. Helena was past saving. They were all past saving.

"No escape," Swordere yelled. "Stupid meat. Working meat. Easy here. Safe here. Food here. Work yes. Try run. Try escape." He shook his head. "No escape. Pain now. Suffer now. Death no. Example meat."

Helena stirred, lifted her head a little. Her mouth worked. She looked so tired, in so much pain. Dien wanted to run to her and... she didn't even know what she could do. The butcher grabbed a water skin, tilted Helena's head back, dribbled some water into her mouth. This was how they did it. They'd keep her alive for as long as possible, draw out her agony, make every moment a torment until her body couldn't take more. It was a game to them, a challenge, how long they could make her live, how much of her they could tear away before her final ember guttered out.

Dien's blood seethed and boiled. She tensed. Roka shook her violently. It was nothing to him. There was nothing Dien could do. The demons were too strong, too brutal.

"Work meat!" Swordere shouted. "Work now."

The thralls were dragged away and put to work. Dien found herself bundled into the forge, working the bellows in Helena's place. Worse, she was opposite Enna Rusk. The older woman wouldn't meet her gaze, only stared at the ground, frowning.

Dien lost herself to the physical exertion. The ache in her gut from pulling on the paddle was welcome. It made her feel like she was doing something.

It felt like punishment.

Around mid-sun, Helena started screaming again. Not a cry for help, just wild, animal terror and pain mixed together into a primal shriek.

They were on a break, waiting for the forge to cool a little to start pumping the bellows again. Dien stepped off the paddle, took a step towards Helena's screams. Karta leapt in front of her, grabbed her by the arm. The other woman was smaller than Dien, but not weak. Still, Dien shrugged her away and glared down at her. Karta stared back, the black Lorekeeper marks around her eyes making her seem fierce.

"Don't," Karta hissed. "There's nothing you can do for her. If you leave your work, they'll only bring you back and find a way to make it worse for her."

"How?" Dien's voice shattered on the word. "How could it be worse for her? They're killing her."

"It can always be worse, Dien," Karta said. "Believe me, they can always make it worse."

"How long?" Dien said. "How long can they keep her like that?"

Karta sighed. "Maybe three days, maybe seven. They'll keep her alive as long as they can. I'm sorry. It... it was a good plan until..."

"Work meat!" the blacksmith shouted from the other side of the forge. "More heat. Pump now."

They hurried back to the bellows and went back to work. Dien stared at Enna Rusk as they dragged the paddle down and then up, down and then up. She fantasised about running into the other room, grabbing her da's old hammer, smashing it into Enna's hateful face.

"Why?" Dien asked as they worked, panting out the words. "Tell me why?"

"Weren't meant to be her," Enna wheezed in between working the bellows. "Were meant to be you, Dien Hostain." She pulled down on the paddle. "All that talk of escape and such. Gonna get us killed. They were meant to take you."

Dien agreed with her on that. She wished they had taken her instead of Helena, though an ugly, guilty part of her was grateful they hadn't. The pain Helena was in; she knew she couldn't take it. No one could.

The thralls were walked back to their cages that night, all of them led past the butchery so they could see again what awaited them if they tried to escape. Helena's lips were moving, but Dien couldn't hear any words. She was shoved on.

Dien huddled in the corner of their cage, wrapped in furs, when the demons brought food. She didn't touch hers, even when Luci held the bowl up to her lips. Dien just turned her head away. She couldn't stomach eating. Especially not when Helena started screaming again. She turned away and buried herself in the furs, trying to hide from the world as if she could pretend she was somewhere else, anywhere else. Back home in her village, snuggled up in her creaky old cot.

She squirmed beneath the furs, trying to get comfortable, and her hand brushed something hard. A bowl. The bowl filled with grease she'd stolen from the butchers. The grease was a congealing mass of gunk, but it was still moist.

Luci lay behind Dien, wrapped her stick thin arms around her just like she had for Helena so many times over the past year to keep her company. Oddly, she was cold as fresh snow, as though she were sucking the heat from Dien.

Dien waited until the dead of night, just as they had planned the day before. It was a struggle. She was so tired. All she wanted to do was close her eyes and sleep. Once the noises of the cages had died down, and the warbling laughs and shouts from the demons had quieted, Dien gripped the bowl of grease and wriggled free from Luci's embrace. The smaller woman rolled over but didn't wake.

Dien slathered grease on the hinges of the cage door, working it into all the gaps. She used most of the bowl, and when it was done, she put her shoulder to the door and pushed. Little by little, it ground open almost silently. She slipped from the cage and stole into the night.

She knew she should run, maybe get the others and see if they could still follow the original plan. Escape via the cave, slip past the monster. But she was certain the demons would have piled rocks in front of the cave by now. Besides, she wasn't trying to escape. She had something more important to do.

Dien crept into the demon camp, hiding in patches of shadow, straining to hear any demons before they found her. Some snored in their pit homes, others patrolled the dusty pathways between tents. Many gathered around the fires, grunting in that language Dien still couldn't understand. She kept a wary distance.

There was a small fire in its dying stages just next to the butchery. The light it cast was a ruddy glow, but it was enough to reveal the demon hound dozing there. Only one of them, the male without the sabrefangs. Dien couldn't see the other. The butcher was nowhere in sight, but Helena was still there, strung up on the line. Her eyes were closed, but Dien could see by the ragged way her chest heaved she was still alive, still breathing.

Dien looked around. There were no demons in sight save for the hound sleeping at the fire. She heard a demon bellow out a laugh, but it was far away, the noise fading quickly. Steeling herself for what had to be done, Dien darted out into the open and crossed the distance to the butchery.

Up close, the stink of blood and offal was even worse. Dien reached Helena and paused. Her belly was cut open, her entrails spilling out, blood both dry and wet all over her skin. Dien knew with a savage certainty there was no saving her friend. She had known it from the moment Helena was taken. That wasn't why she was there.

"Helena," Dien whispered. She touched her friend's leg lightly.

Helena's eyes fluttered open and she drew a ragged, bubbling breath. It took a moment for her to see Dien, then her lips quivered as if she was trying to speak, but there were no words, only a soft murmur.

"I'm sorry," Dien said. "I'm so sorry. I never meant... I'm sorry."

Helena just wheezed. Her eyes flicked to the side and Dien followed her gaze. On the ground, half buried in the stony dirt was a small knife. One of the butcher's blades, dropped and forgotten. Dien bent and picked it up. It was a wicked-looking knife, razor sharp on one side, serrated on the other, and the point curled into a savage hook. Dien gazed up at Helena. Her friend only blinked at her, but it seemed a plea. Permission to do the most horrible thing Dien could imagine.

She reached up, standing on tip toes. "I'm so sorry." She cupped a hand around Helena's cheek. Tears blurred her eyes and her throat tightened until she could barely breathe.

Helena held her gaze and her lips parted just a little. "Freedom," she croaked.

Dien almost broke. But she gathered her courage and gave her friend one last sorry smile. "I love you, Helena Tressel. Goodbye."

Dien gritted her teeth and dragged the blade across Helena's throat. Blood sluiced down her chest, dripped from her skin into the bucket and onto the ground. Her eyes fluttered, her gaze never leaving Dien's, then they slid closed. Dien stood and watched as the friend she had known all her life bled out and died in damning silence.

She dropped the knife, buried her head in bloody hands, bit back the sob that tried to rip itself free. Helena was dead. She deserved so much better, but in the end death was the only mercy Dien could give.

Behind her, taloned claws scuffed the dirt. Dien heard the demon hound snuff loudly, then growl.

Dien turned just as the demon hound leapt at her. She threw herself to the side too slowly and the demon smashed into her, sent her sprawling. She cried out in pain as she cracked her knee on the rocky ground, but immediately started scrambling away. She had to run, get away before the other demons came to investigate the noise. Back to the cage and they might never know it was her.

The hound howled and pounced on her back flattening her against the ground. Sharp stones ground into her cheek and she struggled, flailed. Claws raked down her back, tearing open the thick furs and scoring her skin. Dien writhed and threw back her arm. Her elbow smacked into the demon's muzzle and pain flared as if she'd hit stone, but the weight disappeared from her back.

She heard demons grunting in their own language, rousing from the pits they slept in. She was out of time. Dien surged to her feet and turned just as the demon hound slammed into her again. She hit the ground hard, the air blasted from her lungs, and struggled to draw a breath.

Dien flailed, punching at the hound as it darted in at her. She caught it good in the face, her fist connecting with the demon's eye. It staggered back, yelped, snarled, then lunged at her. Dien raised her hands to block its biting teeth. A taloned claw whipped out and slashed across her face. Dien screamed in agony, gurgled as her throat filled with blood.

"Earta back. No meat. No eat."

Dien coughed blood. She couldn't see anything. She was sure she had her eyes open, but she couldn't see. Her face was a mess of agony. She felt nothing but pain and blood and her own breath bubbling on her ruined lips. The hound had savaged her face. She prayed to the Moons and Sun for death to take her. She could join Helena in cold oblivion.

She heard the hound padding away, snarling, licking its jowls. The sounds of demons laughing came closer. Something grabbed her by her furs and lifted her up. She couldn't see, couldn't smell. She could barely breathe. But she could hear Swordere's voice and it sounded close.

"Stupid meat. No die. Live meat." The demon laughed.

CHAPTER 14

THE FIRST TIME DIEN WOKE EVERYTHING WAS PAIN AND
noise. She was blind. She heard bodies shifting around her, the harsh
laugh of a demon. A hand patted her forehead and a quiet voice whispered something close to her ear, but her mind couldn't make out the
words. She slipped back into unconsciousness.

The next time she woke, her breath caught in her throat and she coughed
weakly. Every breath felt like she was sucking it through pursed lips. Her
face was fire. She couldn't move. Nothing made sense.

"Just rest," said a voice, one she recognized but couldn't place. Her
mind wasn't working right.

"I'm going to pour something into your mouth. Don't panic, Dien."

Something solid was pressed between her ruined lips and the pain
burst to life there.

"Sorry. Sorry. I know it hurts, but you have to eat. Oh, Dien, I'm so
sorry!"

Something warm dribbled into her mouth. She swallowed on

instinct, slowly, painfully. If it had a taste, she couldn't tell. It was soon too much and she choked, spluttered. The darkness smothered her again and she was gone.

"Make live. Keep alive." She knew that voice. Demon. Most hated monster. "No die. She die. You die. Keep alive."

A name formed before her: Swordere. Dien tried to picture the owner. A brutish face, black and red skin, studded with bony horns. Stretched leather screaming, always screaming. Hounds! Dien felt her heart quickening in her chest. She wanted to cry out. Fear gripped hold of her like bony fingers clutching at her insides. Slavering jaws, jagged teeth, talons raking across her face. Pain! So much pain.

"Her wounds are so severe." That was the voice from earlier. Another name shimmered in her mind: Luci. "I don't know if she'll..."

Swordere growled and Dien heard a meaty smack followed by a timid squeak of pain.

"No die. Keep alive. No die. Make eat."

"But it's..."

"Make eat. Keep alive. No die."

Dien heard footsteps storming away, receding into the background noise of the camp. Demonholme, that was what she called it. A place full of nightmares, terrors, pain, and death.

"Here," Luci said. "You have to eat, Dien. I'm sorry. Just swallow it. Don't think."

A bowl was placed against her lips again. It didn't hurt as much as before. She opened them as much as she could, felt liquid dribble down into her mouth again. It was thick and soupy and had stringy chunks in it. She swallowed as much as she could, then let herself go again.

Something soft and damp wiped across Dien's eyelids. She sucked in a rasping breath and coughed. Her throat hurt, but she could breathe easier than before. Her face was new agony, stinging everywhere like angry bees were stabbing at her.

"It's alright, Dien," Luci said. "Some of the swelling has gone down. I'm cleaning your wounds, then I'll wrap the bandages back up."

She tried to speak, to ask how she had survived, but the words stuck in her throat and came out as a guttural hiss.

"Oh dear," Luci said. She wiped the cloth over Dien's eyes again. It felt like sand digging into her skin.

Dien forced a single eyelid open. The light was blinding bright. She couldn't see anything past the white glare. She blinked and blinked and blinked until the light resolved into sunlight streaming in past a fur tent flap. Luci leaned into view, fretting with a damp cloth in hand. She lowered the cloth and Dien felt it washing over her cheek. She gasped from the pain.

"Sorry. I have to wipe away the blood and puss. It's best for your wounds. Oh Dien, you... you..." Luci swallowed hard and looked away. "You'll be fine. I'll see that you are. I won't let you die."

Dien tried to tell her friend that she wanted to die. That she should just let her slip away. But the words stuck in her throat again. Besides, she remembered Swordere telling Luci that if she died, so did Luci. She had no choice then. No choice but to survive for the sake of her friend. Her one remaining friend.

"Hhhhhhhh." Dien groaned and tried to speak.

"Don't try to talk."

She ignored Luci and tried again. "Heeell..." Dien stopped to breathe heavily. Just forcing out a single sound made her feel so weak and tired. Her eyelids were so heavy. "Llleennnna."

"Helena?" Luci asked. She frowned and looked away. "She's dead, Dien." Fat tears rolled down Luci's cheeks. She trembled, buried her face in her hands.

"Guuuuu... d." Dien gave up trying to speak and relaxed back with a heavy sigh.

Luci stopped trembling. She went very still. Slowly, she took her hands from her face and wiped her cheeks. Dien couldn't quite understand, but she almost looked like a different person. Her face was slack, emotionless.

"Here," Luci said in a toneless voice. "You need to eat." She disappeared for a few moments, then reappeared with a bowl.

Dien drank as much of the broth as she could. Her taste was returning and the broth had a thick, meaty flavour to it. Luci watched her with large, empty eyes, then pulled the bowl away.

Dien closed her eye and settled back into sleep.

"How long was I gone?" Dien slurred. She still couldn't speak properly. She hadn't seen the damage the demon hound had done to her face yet, still swathed in bloody bandages, but she could feel it.

"Horn Day came and went three times," Luci said, shifting around the other side of the tent. "You were in and out of consciousness, mumbling a lot, sometimes crying out. Swordere pulled me out of the cages and dragged me here. Told me to make you live." She offered a timid smile.

The tent was small, barely large enough for the two women. It was centred around a depression in the ground, roughly dug but worn smooth by the passage of time. There wasn't much in the tent but a mound of furs, a wooden chest, and the two of them. Dien eyed the chest as she pushed up onto her elbows. Even that meagre effort exhausted her, and she felt the trembling start. Still, she persevered.

"What's in the chest?"

"Herbs mostly. A pestle and mortar, some bowls and cups." Luci shrugged and lifted the chest lid a little. "They're surprisingly proficient herbalists, these demons. There's Kitfeather berries, Heartsbone seeds, Collarshroom root.

"Collarshroom?"

Luci nodded and reached into the chest, pulled out a pale, spongy, knot of root as large as a knuckle. "Chew on this and it will chase away exhaustion, make you feel strong as... a demon. It's a lie though. Once it wears off, you'll barely be able to stand. And here, they even have ragweed."

Dien blinked a single eye at Lucy. Her other eye was still swollen shut, the skin around it shredded by the hound's jagged talons, but Luci assured her the eye was still there.

"Ragweed only grows in the warmth. Even in Berrywhistle, in the height of summer, we struggled to make it grow. Mother spent years trying to get it to flourish in the gardens, but we could never get more than a few roots each year. It's such an odd herb. Does nothing on its own, but mix it right with Blindthistle, and apply the tincture straight to the blood, and it boosts the drowsy effects. I used it on you to keep you unconscious for the first week, didn't want you waking up and pulling your wounds worse with screaming. Or you can mix ragweed with Carrionshade and you have a powder that will make a person shit out everything they've ever eaten." She laughed and then clasped a hand over her mouth.

"Sorry," Luci said around her hand. "That was rude of me, wasn't it?"

Dien just stared at her friend. She might have tried a smile, but her face wasn't up to the task. It might never be. "We're surrounded by demons and I'm half dead, Luci. Sun and Moons, you're allowed to curse. In fact, there's probably never been a more deserving time." Talking took it out of her and she found her face aching and her limbs trembling.

Luci smiled. "My mother used to mix Ragweed and Carrionshade for an expulsive. Watered down, of course, to reduce the effect. Do you remember when Marj Tager accidentally ate those Neverberries?"

Dien nodded. "She said she thought they were Hoodnuts." Just the thought of home both lifted Dien's spirits and cut her to shreds all over again.

"My mother gave her the expulsive. Saved her life."

"She didn't leave the outhouse for three days."

Luci giggled. "I know. She moaned so loud Helena said she thought Old Swiff must be in there with her." Her smile fell away as grief reared its head again.

The tent flap opened and Swordere stood there. His screaming face tunic looked even more horrific in the gloomy light of a foggy winter morning.

"Eat now. Feed meat." He held out a steaming bowl and grinned.

Dien's pulse pounded in her ears. She hated the demon. She hated all demons, but this one, this monster had taken everything from her. She wanted him to pay. She wanted him to die. She wanted to stand over his body, spit on his corpse and tear out his shitty heart.

Luci took the bowl meekly and placed it on the ground. She bowed her head.

Dien made the mistake of looking at Swordere, meeting his black gaze. He leered backed at her. "Live meat. Example meat. No escape. Others know. Meat sees. Working now. No escape." He kicked her in the ribs and Dien doubled over, coughing and spluttering, the pain in her chest setting her face on fire all over again.

"You mustn't..." Luci started but was cut off by a solid smack as Swordere back-handed her.

Swordere turned and walked from the tent. "Eat meat. Live meat. She die. You die." The tent flap closed behind him.

Dien finished coughing and struggled up onto her elbows again. Luci was curled in a ball on the floor, sobbing quietly.

"Luci," Dien slurred. "How bad is it?"

Luci stopped sobbing and went very still. She uncoiled and sat up in a fluid motion. Her upper lip and cheek were split, dribbling blood, but her face was slack.

"That bastard," Dien hissed. "Sun and Moons, Luci, I want to kill him."

Luci cocked her head to the side a little. Blood dripped from her lip into her lap. "You need to eat," she said tonelessly.

Dien tasted the meat in the broth. She couldn't remember eating so well since before being captured. Winter was here which meant it had been a full year already since the demons raided Berrywhistle. She paused halfway through eating and Luci pulled the bowl away from her lips.

"You eat some, Luci. You need it too."

Luci glanced down at the bowl in her hands. "I am not allowed. This food is for you alone, Dien."

"What? Why? What is it?"

Luci met her stare with a flat gaze. "The demons are very cruel."

Dien shook her head, refusing to believe. "What is it, Luci?"

Luci glanced at the bowl again. "It is Helena."

Dien threw up.

"Why?" she asked after emptying her stomach. She could still taste it and the thought made her sick, made her want to throw up again. "How could you?"

Luci just sat there, perfectly still, the bowl cooling in her hands. "Swordere made it very clear. If you do not eat, they kill me. If you die, they kill me. I am to stay by your side and nurse you back to health, or they kill me. I am sorry, Dien. I had no choice." She didn't sound sorry. She didn't sound like anything.

Dien had no choice, either. The demons had made sure of that. Luci was right when she said the demons were very cruel. Either Dien ate the broth—her dead friend—or her living friend died, too. She curled her hands into fists, pounded at the ground, screamed. It earned her nothing.

Dien remembered a time back in Berrywhistle, when the Ruger sisters had called her ugly and pushed her down in the mud, threw crawlers in her hair and down her dress. They'd called her a bog witch, all because she'd been staring at Panyet and Tinsy Ruger liked him. Dien had been ten years old and she'd run home crying. When her da had found her, crying in his tool closet, she shouted at him that she hated the sisters.

He'd waited until she cried herself hoarse, then reached up and pulled his big hammer from its mounting, the one he always cleaned and polished, but never used. The one now rusting in the smith demon's forge.

"Hate is like this hammer, little bug," he'd said. "It's a useful tool, when something needs hammering. But useless when what you actually need is to saw a plank in two or carve out a dovetail joint. It has its place, has its purpose. But the thing is…"

He held out the hammer. Dien had never been allowed to touch it before and she reached for it eagerly. He dropped it into her hands and she staggered from the weight of it.

"Heavy, isn't it? And the longer you carry it, the heavier it gets, and the more it starts to look like a saw, a knife, a chisel, whatever you need. But it's still just a hammer. And all it's really good for is driving nails into wood."

Dien knew why that memory came to her now. She hated the demons, Swordere most of all. But that hate wouldn't serve her purpose. She didn't need a hammer. She needed to think clearly.

Dien picked up the bowl of broth. There were strands of meat floating in the brown soup. Strands of Helena. She almost retched but swallowed it down. "If I don't eat, they kill you?"

Luci nodded calmly, still and emotionless.

Dien raised the bowl to her lips and slurped it down. It was the most vile thing she had ever tasted. When she was done, she threw the bowl across the tent. She was angry and wanted to scream, to rage. She was exhausted and wanted to sleep. She did neither of those things. Instead, she gestured to the wooden chest.

"Ragweed and Carrionshade. You have both in that chest?"

CHAPTER 15

HORN DAY ROLLED AROUND A FOURTH TIME BEFORE DIEN was recovered enough to stand. Swordere was impatient.

"Her wounds are mostly healed," Luci said, keeping her gaze down. She was wringing her hands, voice trembling. "They'll scar, like you wanted. But she should keep them bandaged for a while to make sure they don't get infected."

Swordere growled and Luci cowered. "No cover. Weak meat. Scarred meat. Example weak. Others see. Others know. Meat understands. No escape. No defy. Weak meat. All meat. Weak thralls."

The demon crouched down before Dien. She stared into his mottled, horned face. "No cover." He reached out and she didn't flinch back. Swordere grabbed a handful of the bandages and wrenched them from Dien's face. Her skin burned from the cold, itched. She felt some of her wounds weeping still.

Swordere laughed. He stalked out of the tent.

Dien gingerly touched a hand to her face. The wounds stung. The flesh was raw, raised, and ragged. Luci pushed a bowl of water towards her and Dien stared into it. As the waters stilled, she saw the ruin of her face. Three great rents slashed across her burnt sand skin. The first started at her cheek, ran across her left eye, ended at her hairline. The hair just above it was losing its colour, turning white. The second gash ran from her jaw, across her nose and onto her cheek. She thought it a miracle she hadn't lost her nose. The third wound ran up from her chin and split her bottom lip in two. The flesh was healing, but it would be forever ruined. She would bear horrific scars, the proof of her failure, for the rest of her life.

That night, Swordere came for them. They heard the demon coming and Luci pressed something into Dien's hand. It was the Collarshroom root, thick and white and spongy. Dien shoved it in her mouth and chewed. It chased away her exhaustion, made her feel strong. Strong enough to stand and walk, at least.

Swordere wrenched open the tent flap and pulled them out and shoved them on. They were going back to the cages. The hounds stalked along beside them. Dien stared at the male hound, the one without the sabre teeth. She still remembered the flash of its claws at it raked across her face. She found herself trembling and had to look away from the hound lest her knees turn liquid.

The cages were the same, and yet also different. The black iron bars were as before, but the cages seemed more hostile. Helena was gone and with her went the warmth the thralls had shared. Karta and Gartlen had changed cages, joined Samir in the cell he had once shared with Dien and Luci and Helena. Enna Rusk had swapped, too. She huddled in the corner of Donnel's cage, a fearful look on her face. Dien wondered what the woman had traded for the safety of Donnel and his cronies.

Swordere stopped behind Dien and grabbed a handful of her hair. The demon wrenched her head back and waved a torch in front of her face, making sure all the thralls got a good look at her.

"Example meat. Scarred meat. No escape. Weak thralls. Working meat." He pulled the torch away and gave Dien a shove. She stumbled and fell to her knees on the rocky ground, panting.

She was so exhausted. The Collarshroom had chased away the weakness, but she knew it was a lie. But she couldn't give in yet. Her ordeal wasn't over.

Swordere pulled open the doors to the cages. "In meat."

Luci was the first to move. She kept her head down, hands curled before her and walked into the cage with Samir and the others. Dien staggered back to her feet, squared her shoulders, and walked into Donnel's cage.

Enna gasped but Donnel laughed as Swordere pushed the cages shut behind her, the door squealing like a pig on butcher's block.

"Sun and Moons, Dien Hostain," Donnel said, grinning through his grimy beard. "You weren't pretty before, but now your face makes a bloody arsehole look inviting, it does." His cronies laughed.

Dien ignored them, her gaze was locked on Enna. The woman was as responsible for Helena's death as Swordere. Her vengeance started here. Dien took a menacing step forward, hands bunched into fists, the false energy of the Collarshroom pounding through her burning blood.

Enna scrambled to her feet. "Help me, Donnel."

"Help yourself," Donnel sneered.

Enna stared hard at Dien. "You're the one who..."

Dien launched herself at the woman with a cry of fury. She hit her in the stomach, knocked Enna back against the rocky wall of the cage. The other woman cried out in pain, pushed at Dien feebly. Dien wrenched her around and threw her to the ground.

Sometimes, a hammer was exactly the tool you need and hatred was making Dien's blood boil, giving her strength. She fell on Enna and they wrestled there among the dirt and rocks. Enna struck Dien in the face, an elbow to the chin, then put her hand on Dien's cheek and tried to push her away.

Donnel and his cronies cheered. "Do something proper," Donnel shouted. "One of you hit the other one."

Dien heard Samir shouting as well, but the thunder in her ears drowned out the words.

She slipped away from Enna's hand against her cheek and a finger hooked into her mouth. Dien bit down hard. Blood washed into her mouth. Enna screamed in terrified pain, tried to pull free. Dien bit harder, teeth mashing flesh and gristle. She gnawed like a dog with a bone, wrenching this way and that.

"Shit!" Donnel said, no longer cheering. "Get her off."

Dien wrestled with Enna, got on top of her, still biting down on her finger. She reached inside her furs, pulled out the little reed pouch Luci had prepared and shoved it in the other woman's mouth. Enna coughed, but Dien shoved her hand under her chin and forced her mouth closed. Enna choked on her screams and swallowed involuntarily.

Hands hooked underneath Dien's arms at the same time she bit through Enna's finger entirely. Enna reeled away, screaming, clutching her hand as blood gushed from the stump of a finger. Dien threw an elbow into the face of the person behind her. She heard a cry of pain and one of her arms came free. A small fist-sized rock rolled to a stop at her feet and she snatched it, spun about and slammed it into the side of another man's head.

Donnel and five of his cronies faced her, all men, all larger than her. They didn't matter. Just as long as they didn't stop her in time. Demons shouted and torches bobbed in the distance as they came to see what was happening.

Dien turned and sprang at Enna again. The other woman tried to get her uninjured hand up, but Dien knocked it away and smacked the rock down into Enna's face once, twice, a third time. Enna went limp and Dien hit her again and again.

More hands grabbed Dien from behind. She tried to swing her rock at them, but another hand grabbed hold of her wrist. She kicked out, flailed, but Donnel's cronies had hold of her.

"Put her down," Donnel snarled.

Dien slammed a knee into a man's groin and he fell away with a mewl of pain. She twisted free of the other pair of hands and leapt at Enna again. The woman's face was even more of a ruin than her own. Blood bubbled weakly between lips. It wasn't enough. Dien had lost her rock, but she punched Enna in the face twice before she heard the squeal of the gate opening.

Swordere wrenched her up and away. Dien panted, sweated, trembled, at the limits of her strength. The false energy of the Collarshroom was vanishing quickly and not even hatred could carry her any further. She knew there was no point struggling against a demon. It didn't matter. She had done what she needed to. Swordere slammed her against the bars of the cage, his dark stare furious. He glanced down at Enna's body, nudged her with his clawed foot. She didn't move. There wasn't even breath bubbling the blood between her lips anymore. Enna Rusk was already dead.

Swordere bent and scooped up Enna's body like a dropped sock. The demon tossed it outside of the cages. "Eira come. Earta come." The demon hounds loped out from the foggy darkness. "Eat meat."

Both hounds pounced on Enna's body and started tearing into it, gouging out the soft bits. Just as Dien had thought, the hounds went straight for the stomach and intestines. Just like they had when they tore apart her mother. Mindless beasts, as predictable as they were savage.

Swordere glanced around the thralls from inside the cage. They all cowered from him. All except Dien. She faced him, met his cruel gaze. "No fight. Wasted meat," Swordere said. He turned and walked out the cage, pulling the door squealing shut behind him.

Swordere walked back towards the camp. He pointed at Enna's mangled corpse and snapped some words in their demonic language. One of the other demons snarled at the hounds until they backed away, then scooped up Enna's body and followed Swordere. The hounds snarled for a moment, then continued gulping down Enna's innards. Dien could only hope they both got a taste of the herbal mixture she had made Enna swallow.

She spat Enna's severed finger into her hand and gripped it tight in her fist. The blood was thick and oily in her mouth, made her want to throw up. She leaned back against the wall and sighed. She had just murdered Enna. Dien shoved down the guilt that threatened to swallow her. Enna had deserved it; she was responsible for what had happened to Helena. Even so, it was a horrible thing she had done. She threw up then, and most of it was blood, none of it hers.

"At first I thought you were brave," Gartlen said from close by. Dien opened her eyes and saw him crouched at the bars between their cages. "Now I know it was just stupidity. Fire's Light, Dien, what were you trying to achieve?"

Dien laughed bitterly. What was she trying to achieve? The same thing she had been from the moment the demons took her. Freedom. And now revenge, too.

"Thank you for throwing me the rock," she said.

Gartlen snorted. "Only thing I could do. I can't protect you in that cage, Dien."

She shot him a wan smile. "I don't need protecting. I'm right where I need to be."

Dien closed her eyes and rested for a bit. She had achieved everything she needed to. Enna was dead and the hounds had swallowed the herbs. Everything else could wait.

They all ate Enna Rusk that night. Most of the thralls ate her in bowls of broth. Dien pushed her own bowl away, not caring which of Donnel's cronies got their second helpings. She sat in the corner of the cage, so that her friends were at her back, and she gnawed the skin and flesh away from Enna's severed finger, spitting out ragged chunks, until she had two small bones to work with. Then she picked up a stone and started shaving away at the bones just like she had done at her mother's feet so many times back in the village, filing them into sharp, needly points.

CHAPTER 16

The first night back in the cages passed without incident. Dien tried to stay awake, to keep an eye on her fellow thralls, but her exhaustion overcame her. She woke with the sun and Gartlen shaking her through the bars at her back. Donnel was already up and watching her, an ugly hunger in his eyes.

Dien was taken to the forge that day to work the bellows alongside Karta, Narcy, and another woman. She felt the wounds on her back weeping with every pull on the paddle, the scars on her face stretching with every grimace of effort. Narcy watched Dien with a wide-eyed look that might have been fear or respect. Dien didn't care which, only that the grumpy woman didn't try to slack at her work. She doubted she had the strength to work the paddle alone.

Her plan appeared to be working. The two demon hounds were sick. The male loped about near the butcher, whining all day. It had the stink of offal about it and would not eat, even when the butcher tried to give it the choicest cuts of meat. The female was nowhere to be seen. Dien trudged back to the cages that day with a savage feeling of victory. But she could not be sure the hounds would be sick for more than a few days. Her time was limited.

Even as the thralls reached the cages, a brutal wailing howl sounded from the camp. It was a terrible scream full of rage and grief. It did not come from either of the hounds, but from Swordere. One of the demon hounds was dead. Dien hoped it would be passed off as an illness, but she could not be sure Swordere wouldn't suspect her.

When Roka pulled open the cage doors, Dien didn't hesitate. She walked straight into the bear's den, into Donnel's cage. It was not for want, but for need. If Swordere came for her, he would punish those close to her first, to further make an example of her. If she could spare them that she would, even if it meant risking another night with Donnel.

Once the food had been delivered, Roka didn't leave. The demon settled close to the cages, playing with a small curve of metal that he could pick at to make twanging noises. It seemed the demons were no longer leaving the thralls unwatched.

The freezing fog rolled in thicker that night, pouring from the mountaintops. Gartlen sat on the other side of the bars, his back to Dien's. "Donnel will come for you tonight," he whispered.

Dien worked at the little bone needles. She'd scraped one into a fine point and was using the edge on the other to work a little groove into the length. It was fine, laborious work, but she couldn't snap the needle. She had no more fingers to bite off to fashion more.

"I know," she rasped. Her voice had not yet recovered from the mauling by the hound. It sounded strange and gravelly.

"You should have come back to our cage."

Dien looked up and met Donnel's gaze. He didn't look away. "I couldn't risk it," she said softly. "You should keep your distance. If Swordere comes for me, make him think you hate me. But thank you for caring."

Gartlen looked away. "I don't know what you mean, I'm just looking out for them. Worried what you'll do to them if they attack you."

She kept working at the bone needle until her hands slipped and her eyelids fell closed.

Dien woke with a start at a sharp pinch on her arse. She opened her eyes to see Donnel reaching for her. On pure instinct she lashed out, jammed her thumb into his eye. He recoiled, yelling in pain, clutching at his face.

"Up, Dien. Get up," Gartlen hissed.

Dien hauled herself up and felt a rock pressed into her hand from behind. She brandished it even as Donnel thrashed about.

"Don't just stand there," Donnel snarled. "Get her!"

Two of his cronies started towards her, but Dien raised the rock as threateningly as she could. "First of you to come close goes the same way as Enna," she shouted. "You think your friends will hesitate? You think Donnel won't happily eat you?"

The advancing thralls faltered, glanced warily at each other. Dien realised that they didn't trust each other. They were held together by Donnel, by his strength and his will, but they had been robbed of order and laws for so long that each of them knew they were one bad slip or injury away from being the next meal. They looked to Donnel because they thought he was a leader, but he only cared for himself and inspired that same selfishness in those who followed him. A wary alliance based on fear rather than friendship. A weak alliance.

"Stupid meat," Roka banged his black knife against the bars. "No fight. Sleep meat." The demon turned around and grumbled as he walked back to his spot.

Donnel crawled to the far end of the cage and glared at Dien with his one remaining eye, his other had already swollen shut and was weeping blood. She sat back down but kept her rock close.

"Well done," Gartlen whispered through the bars.

"Did you pinch my arse?" Dien asked.

"Woke you up, didn't it?" He chuckled, but it was as brief as an ember touching snow. "Next time they'll come at you all at once."

"There won't be a next time," Dien said. "I'm going to take them from him."

Gartlen laughed again. "Fire's Light, Dien, you've got balls an ox would be proud of."

She reached behind, slipped her hand through the bars and found Gartlen's. She gave his fingers a squeeze. "Thank you. Give this to Luci.

She knows what to do." Dien slipped the bone needle with the groove down its length into Gartlen's palm.

Gartlen's hand lingered on her own for a few moments. Warm and comforting, calloused from hard work, but strong, reliable. Part of her wished he'd hold on, wind his fingers through hers and not let go. She wanted to feel that connection, to feel close to someone. She wanted to feel anything but the pain.

"What are you planning, Dien?" His breath stirred her hair.

"Escape," she whispered.

It was only partly a lie. She did want to escape. But there was something she wanted even more. She wanted to kill the demons. She wanted to kill every single one of them.

The next day passed in a blur. Dien pumped the bellows with a singular focus and Karta regularly had to tell her to slow down. It was tough. She was eager, ready, filled with a nervous energy. Tonight she'd make the demons pay, and she'd get her friends out.

Eira, the hound was dead. Swordere burned the body and howled about it throughout the day. His grief was nothing to Dien. He had murdered her mother, fed her to his hounds. He had slaughtered Helena and forced Dien to consume her. He could shriek to the Sun and the Moons and Dien would not soften. She would see him die screaming.

Earta, the other hound, had not died. The beast was still sick, still vomiting and shitting itself throughout the day, but it clung to life. Dien knew her time was limited. They needed to escape before the hound recovered or it would track them. Even then, she did not know how long their trail would last, how many days cold could the demon could track them.

The fog was so thick that evening Dien could stir it with her hand. It twirled in lazy patterns and chilled the skin but seemed almost fortuitous. She could ask for no better cover to escape. Perhaps the Moons and Sun had had their fill of her suffering and were now smiling upon her.

She waited until after the thralls had been fed. Until the demons had retreated back to their camp. Roka was left on guard again. The bug-eyed demon grumbled and hissed about the job.

Dien stood. Everyone in her cage watched. Donnel's one eye was filled with rage, but the rest of the thralls looked uncertain. Dien turned to find Luci in the other cage.

Something disturbed the air above them, sending fog swirling down in flurries. It almost sounded like a bird whooshing past on feathery wings. It was quickly followed by another, and then silence. Whatever it was, it didn't matter. It was time for Dien to get them out. Luci, Gartlen, Karta, and Samir.

And all the others, too.

Dien turned back to Luci. "Are you ready?"

Luci nodded and pulled her bowl close, wiped it clean with a fur, then spat into it. She pulled a reed pouch from her clothes and ripped it open, sprinkling the powder inside into the bowl and mixing furiously with her spittle. Then she fumbled with the needle Dien had made.

Another whoosh above stirred the freezing fog. Dien heard a distant shout, muffled by the mist. There was no time to reason it out. It was up to her now.

"My da…" Her voice broke and she had to clear her throat before she continued. She raised her voice so all the thralls could hear her. "My da told me real strength doesn't come from the arms or from any muscle. It comes from the spirit. It comes from the will to do what is right. He said it comes from having the guts to stand there and say *no* even when someone is beating on you, screaming at you to say *yes*. My da said he knew from both sides that being good to those who mean you harm isn't real strength but being willing to stand up and say no more even under threat… that's strong."

"Your da was a demon loving traitor," Donnel said, rising to his feet.

Dien pointed at Donnel. "You follow him because you don't think you have another choice. Because you think he is strong, that he can get you through this."

"Quiet meat!" Roka shouted out from the foggy darkness.

"You follow a coward," Dien said, raising her raspy voice. "A man who went out of his way to settle a pointless grudge even as demons murdered his family. A man who would attack a woman in her sleep."

Donnel took a menacing step forward. "You be quiet, Dien Hostain, you hear?"

"A man who doesn't care about any of you. Who will call you friend one day then devour your corpse the next. You follow a coward and it makes you all cowards!"

"Stupid meat. Quiet meat," Roka yelled.

There were more shouts drifting out of the fog now, mixed with sounds like the forge at work, metal striking metal.

"Are you content with cowering here in fear, waiting to see which of you will be taken next, killed next, eaten next? Are you happy with being no better than beasts, worked and bred and slaughtered? Or are you willing to be better than this coward? Are you willing to stand up and say NO MORE?

"I mean to escape," she stared at them. Even Donnel snarling at her. "This coward won't stop me. The demons won't break me. I will escape. Are you willing to join me? Are you willing to fight for your freedom?"

"You think..." Donnel started but was interrupted by one of his cronies stepping past him.

The man was older, heavily wrinkled with grey hair in tight braids and a crooked nose. He shook his head sadly. "Can't fight them, girl. Can't win. Demons can't be killed. They're immortal."

Dien met his gaze. "Are they?"

She walked to the cage door, pressed her shoulder against it and heaved. The hinges squealed as she forced it open. She heard gasps behind her. Dien slipped through the opening.

"No meat. No escape. Stupid meat." Roka came striding through the dark fog, his eyes wide and furious. He saw Dien standing outside the cages, lumbered towards her, reaching. She dodged to the side, under his grasping claw. Roka followed her, darting quickly in and grabbing her throat. She felt the pressure as he gripped her neck, felt him cut off her air. She met his gaze and matched fury with fury.

Everyone was watching. Roka drew his black knife and raised it to her face.

Behind Roka, Dien saw Luci slink forwards, out of the fog. She reached through the bars, swift as a hare, and jabbed the bone needle into his neck.

Roka cried out and staggered away from the cages, carrying Dien with him, her feet barely touching the ground. He hissed and swayed.

"Stupid meat. Dead... meat. Dea... m-me."

Roka shook his head and stumbled. Dien's feet touched the rocky ground and his grip loosened around his neck. She sucked in a grateful breath of icy air. Roka pawed at his neck, but only succeeded in pushing the needle deeper. His dagger clattered to the ground and his bug eyes drifted shut as the concoction of Ragweed and Blindthistle took effect. With one final grunt, Roka toppled forwards and hit the ground, unconscious.

Another whoosh sped overhead, disturbing the fog. The shouts coming from the camp were louder now and orange smears lit the fog from the camp. There was no turning back. A demon dead, no chance to hide it. All Dien needed, was to convince the thralls to join her.

The thralls were at the cage bars now, watching. Not just her friends, not just Donnel's cronies. All of them.

"They're not immortal," Dien growled. She bent down and picked up Roka's fallen dagger, then plunged it into the demon's neck and ripped it to the side. Blood spurted, gushed. The demon spasmed a few times, then fell still, a spreading pool of red leaking out around him.

"Nothing is immortal," Dien said. She held up the knife to show them the blood on it, then threw it to the ground in angry disdain. She ran to each of the cages in turn and grabbed the doors, wrenching them open, heedless of the loud squeals.

Slowly, the thralls crept from the cages. Some stared closely at Roka's corpse, as if afraid he would lurch upright and attack, others gawked towards the camp. Others still looked up into the misty night. Dien stood before them.

"None of you need stay here. You can all leave. Be better than beasts,

better than demons. You can be human again. You can be free again."
She turned her back on them and stared towards the camp, the fiery
smears lighting it, and the sounds of battle. They could all leave. But
not her.

"Coward, am I?" Donnel said.

Dien turned to find the man crouching by Roka's body. His hand
wrapped around the black iron knife and he stood, advanced on her.

"You are a coward, Donnel," Dien said, meeting his gaze and refusing
to show fear despite her racing heart. "You've always been a coward. You
attacked my father in the dead of night, three of you and armed. You beat
him even when he refused to fight back.

"And here we are now. I am trying to free these people and you stand
there with a knife and threaten me. I name you coward, Donnel Ocha.
But you will find I am *not* my father and I *will* fight back!"

Donnel raised the knife to strike. The grey-haired man from before
grabbed Donnel's arm, wrenched it back.

"What are you doin?" Donnel snarled, flailed at the man with his free
hand.

Another of his cronies rushed forward, grabbed Donnel's other arm,
twisted it behind his back.

"You'll pay for this, Dien Hostain. No better than your demon-
lovin' da."

Luci reared up behind Donnel, a large rock held in both her hands.
She slammed it down on the back of his head with a sickening crunch.
The two men let go his arms and Donnel pitched forwards face first,
unconscious and bleeding on the ground.

Luci stood, the rock held in both hands. Her face was slack, her voice
toneless. "He was going to kill you," she said. "I will never let anyone
hurt you, Dien."

Luci raised the rock again and threw it down with all her strength at
Donnel's head, cracking it open like a bad egg. His body twitched and he
went still. Luci looked up from the corpse she had made and Dien
realised it was not her first.

Dien held her friend's unwavering gaze, then glanced at Donnel's body. A grim smile stretched her lips. "Die in shame, Donnel Ocha."

She would spend no more time on a stupid corpse, Dien looked up towards the gathering thralls. Samir, Karta, and Gartlen waited with them. Dien went to them.

"Get them out of here," she said to Gartlen. "Over the mountains, to the west, just as we planned."

Gartlen nodded, his eyes wide and awestruck, but Samir took a step forward and grabbed Dien by the arm. "What about you?"

Dien gave the old trader a smile, despite her ruined face. "I'm going to make sure they can't follow you. One of the hounds still lives. It can track you. I need to kill it."

"You can't..."

"I *need* to kill it, Samir," Dien said, her voice trembling. She held his gaze a moment longer. "And Swordere, too."

"Don't be stupid Dien," Samir hissed, his hand tightening around her arm. "You might have killed Roka with trickery, but Swordere is different. You don't stand a chance. He will slaughter you."

Dien wrenched her arm free from his grip. She took a step away from him, away from all of them, and smiled.

"My da said a man's consequences are his shadow. Sometimes it's before him and sometimes behind, but it's always there waiting. It's time Swordere met his shadow."

CHAPTER 17

DIEN STRUCK OUT TOWARDS THE CAMP AND THE SOUNDS OF fighting. Luci quickly followed, slinking through the fog behind her.

"What are you doing?" Dien asked.

"Where you go, I go," Luci said. "I cannot protect you if I run away."

Dien considered trying to send her away again, but she couldn't see how. She'd just have to hope Luci ran after seeing her fall.

They skirted the forest and made for the camp via the butchery. Dien had a plan, and the first stop was the forge. She needed a weapon. She needed her father's hammer. Then they needed to kill the surviving hound so it couldn't track the other thralls' escape.

The sounds of battle grew fiercer. Shouts from the demons echoed through the fog. Other voices, too. Voices too clear and harmonious to belong to demons. Judging by the roaring flames and the heat, the thick smoke mixing with the fog, and the orange smear across the camp, most of the tents had to be on fire. Dien felt her blood blazing, burning through her veins.

The first body they came across belonged to a demon, its head clove in two, blood leaking out. It was a tall one, gangly with swirling blue patterns across pale skin, horns jutting from its scalp.

They ran on, past burning tents. The butcher staggered out before them. The huge demon had a cleaver in one hand, his other ending in a bloody stump. Flames blew across Dien's vision and she crouched back, waved Luci to stay down.

They watched as the butcher roared and swung his cleaver. A giant of a man covered head to toe in bronze armour met the cleaver with a shining white sword with frost streaming from the blade. He shouted and pushed the butcher back, then swiped his blade sideways. It bit deep into the butcher's side and the demon screamed.

"You will fall, beast," the man bellowed, his voice echoing from within his helmet. Dien saw then what she had missed before; the man in armour had wings. Huge, grey feathered wings couched high on his back.

Bloody ice crystals burst from where the winged man's sword bit into the butcher's side. The winged man pushed forward and tried to pull his sword free, but the butcher clamped his bloody stump down on it, pinning the blade in his side even as his blood exploded into ice crystals and rime grew over his skin. His cleaver rose and fell, bit into the winged man's neck, punching through his armour. Both demon and winged man collapsed to their knees. They died together, surrounded by flames.

Dien almost ran to investigate, but Luci pulled her away. "It's too hot," her friend said.

The flames were already licking at the butcher's feet and Dien knew there was no way she'd get close enough to investigate. "Did you see... Did that man have wings?"

Luci nodded.

They ran on, skirting the burning tents and the two figures locked in a morbid embrace. The butchery was also on fire, flames pouring from the hut. For so long it had been a place of terror. A place where Dien had seen people strung up, cut open, tortured, and murdered. Now it was an inferno that stank of death.

A flap of huge wings above and Dien and Luci ducked just as another of the winged men soared over head. The flames trailed after him, drawn by his passage. He landed not ten paces away and twirled a glowing golden spear in his hand. The smith charged out of the fog, a giant axe in one hand, and a great hammer in the other. Axe met spear in a shower of sparks and the winged man leapt away, beating his wings. The smith followed, swinging both weapons with ferocity.

"That's my da's hammer?" Dien said. She stood and took a step towards the battle.

The man's armour was a vibrant silvery green, shining brightly in the flames. The smith's skin was pale and mottled. And their weapons crashed together like thunder.

Luci grabbed Dien's arm. "The butchery."

"He has my da's hammer, Luci!" Dien frowned, her scars pulling, then it dawned on her. "The oil!"

They both turned and ran.

An explosion shook the camp, throwing them both to the ground.

Dien shook her head, trying to clear the dancing lights. Black smoke plumed in thick clouds all around making her cough. She couldn't tell where she was, everything was fog and flames. Luci groaned and Dien reached down, hauled her friend back to her feet. She was bleeding from a cut on her forehead.

"I... I don't like it here, Dien," Luci said, no longer speaking in that odd flat tone. "We should go. Please."

Dien shook her head. "Not until we know the hound is dead." She had to shout to be heard over the roaring flames. She looked around for the smith, for his body, for the hammer. There was no sign.

Luci trembled. She clutched Roka's black dagger tight with both hands. "This is all the distraction we need. Let's go."

"No!" Dien snarled. "I am not leaving until Swordere is dead. If you want to go, Luci, then go!"

She shoved her friend away. Luci stumbled a couple of paces, then stopped, still clutching Roka's dagger, eyes wide. It wasn't about escape anymore, not for Dien. She wanted revenge. She needed vengeance. Swordere had taken so much from her, heaped suffering upon her until any sane person would have broken. Until the demon was dead, Dien would never know a moment's peace.

A man in grey armour strode from the flames. He was huge, even bigger than the largest of demons. His black wings were raised away from the fires and he carried a bloodied white sword in hand. He stopped and turned to look at Dien. She could see nothing of his face, so shadowed it was by the helm he wore.

The winged man reached a gauntleted hand towards them. "You…"

The demon hound hit the man from behind, crashing into him and sending him tumbling to the ground. They thrashed around for a few seconds, the hound biting at the man's wings, the man trying to throw the demon off.

Swordere stalked out of the flames next. He stopped and glanced at Dien and Luci. His face twisted into a horrific snarl, made worse by the red and black patterning and blood dripping from the horn on his chin.

"Earta come," Swordere growled.

The demon hound sprang from the winged man's back. He immediately rolled back to his feet, favouring one side, his wing bent and bleeding. Earta padded across the burning ground to Swordere's side. The demon patted the hound's head lovingly, then pointed at Dien and Luci. "Eat meat." With that, he hefted his sword and whip and stalked towards the winged man.

Earta pounced. Dien pushed Luci to the side and leapt the other way. The hound hit the ground between them, spinning quickly. Luci screamed. Earta charged her, pinning her to the ground, claws tearing through fur and scoring flesh.

Dien hesitated, torn between the need to help her friend, and the burning drive to see her vengeance made manifest. The winged man and Swordere clashed, their swords colliding. Each blow was a thunderclap that blasted away dirt and shredded the fog. Luci scrambled beneath the hound as it ripped away swathes of her furs, trying to find flesh beneath. Dien screamed in frustration. She had to save her friend.

She ran at the hound and leapt onto its back. Punching it, she tore out clumps of its hair, dug fingers into its mangy, bleeding skin. One of the horns along its back came free and she flipped it around, plunged it point-first into the monster's chest. The hound bucked and reared and threw her off. Dien hit the ground hard, rolled to a stop.

Dien glanced over to where the winged man and Swordere were fighting. The winged man was dragging one leg, trying to hold his sword up. Swordere lashed his whip back and forth, each crack ringing against the winged man's grey armour, tearing feathers from his wings. The demon was laughing as he pulled the winged man apart piece by piece.

There was a sword at Dien's feet. One of the serrated black ones the smith had been making for the past year. She crouched down and wrapped her hands around the hilt. It was so hot it burned her skin, sent agony racing up her arms. She raised the blade and ran at Earta as the hound pounced on Luci again. Luci screamed in terror and Dien roared at the hound. She raised the sword in both hands and brought it down as hard as she could. The blade sliced a deep gouge in Earta's flank and the hound yelped and leapt away.

Earta limped, circled Dien, snarling at her. Dien tried to keep the sword between her and the hound, but it was so heavy, the blade kept wavering in her hands. Beyond the hound, she could see the winged man down on his knees. Swordere had his whip coiled around the man's neck, underneath his armour, choking him.

Luci leapt out of the burning fog in silence and landed on Earta's back. She plunged her stolen dagger into the hound's neck, pulled it out in a spray of blood, plunged it in again. Earta thrashed about, bucked, reared, but Luci held on, stabbing over and over again. She met Dien's gaze just for a moment. "Go!" she screamed.

Dien turned and ran. She leapt through a patch of fire and charged at Swordere, raised the black sword in both hands.

"Die foe," Swordere hissed down into the face of the winged man.

Dien struck. She put all her weight and will into the strike and drove the black blade up through one of the screaming mouths of Swordere's tunic, through his back, and out the other side.

Swordere reared back, bellowed in pain. He turned, reaching for Dien, but she held onto the sword and was dragged around behind him. She caught her feet on a rock, tripped, and lost her grip.

Dien rolled on the burning ground as Swordere turned towards her. The blade was through his chest, but it didn't even slow him down as he stalked towards her.

A whistle and *thunk* and something smacked into Swordere's head, sending him stumbling. Karta stood just a dozen paces away, backlit by fire, already twirling a sling to send a second rock at the demon.

Swordere roared in anger and raised an arm to block the next rock. It thudded against his chest and he reached for Dien again. She scrambled back away from him.

Gartlen came running out of the smoke and fog, crouching low, a huge shining white sword dragging behind him. He shouted as he slid to a stop and pivoted the sword up and over his shoulder, then down. The blade bit into Swordere's arm, severing his hand.

Gartlen laughed and danced back a step. "Looks like you needed a h—"

Swordere swung his bloody stump and smacked Gartlen in the face, sending him careening away. Even with a sword through his chest and one hand severed, the demon still stood stronger than them all. Another rock whistled through the air and smacked him in the head. It barely fazed him.

Dien scrambled back further and her hands found wood. She glanced down and saw her da's hammer. The wooden haft was scorched, the metal head was rusty and spotted with blood, but Dien would know the weapon anywhere. So many times, she'd watched her da lift it from its bracket with a weary reverence. So many times, she'd seen him clean it, oil it, or sometimes just hold it.

Samir roared as he ran out of the smoke and leapt over Dien. The old trader carried a demon's axe and swung it as though Swordere was a tree needed felling. The axe bit deep into the demon's thigh and he finally went down, dragging it from Samir's hands as he fell.

Swordere writhed on the ground, bleeding from his leg, his arm, his chest. But still clinging to life.

Dien hauled herself back to her feet and dragged her da's hammer with her. She felt him with her then, his big hands on her shoulders, calling her *little bug*, telling her violence was never the answer.

She stared down at the demon who had tormented them for so long, who had caused her so much pain. He had taken everything from her. She hated him. And while she might be her da's daughter, she was not him. For her, violence was the only answer.

"Weak mea—"

Dien swung the hammer up and brought it down on Swordere's head with a resounding crack.

It was over. Finally over. She had her vengeance.

It wasn't enough. It did not fill the void inside of her. It was a drop in the bucket.

Samir panted, knelt by the dead demon, trying to catch his breath. Karta crept from the smoke, approaching as warily as a rabbit expecting a trap. Gartlen lay sprawled on the ground and Dien held out a hand, hauled him to his feet. They had all come back. Despite ordering them to run, they had returned. For her. They had come back for her. Tears welled in Dien's eyes and her heart thundered. She was so glad, even as she cursed them all for fools for following her.

She glanced over to Luci. Earta was down, dead. Luci knelt over the demon hound, still stabbing it with her stolen dagger over and over.

Dien staggered, almost collapsed, used her da's hammer to steady herself. Her hammer. The vessel of her vengeance. She was exhausted. Her arms trembled, her legs ached, her scars felt both too hot and too cold at once.

The winged man uncoiled the whip from around his neck, gasped in a lungful of air, panting. His helmet turned toward her, the black depths strange and unnerving as though he didn't have a face.

"Are you her?" the man croaked, his voice reverent. He raised his helm to the sky. "Brother," he shouted. "I've found her."

Thunder rumbled across the black sky, echoing around the smoky fog. A brief flash of light and something shiny hurtled from the clouds and struck the earth a dozen paces away. Dien peered at it. It was a white sword, fallen from the sky. It had a wide blade, gold symbols running down the centre, and a rounded feathery design for a cross guard.

Lightning crackled around the blade, then flashed blinding brilliance. When Dien's vision cleared, another of the armour-clad winged men knelt there. Lightning traced glowing lines down his golden armour. His wings were the silver of polished steel. When he stood, she saw he was a giant, easily twice as tall as her. His face was hidden within the darkness of his helm, but his eyes blazed as blue as sunlight striking a sapphire.

"Mertral," the newcomer said, his voice rich and warm like a welcome fire on a frosty night. "Are you well?" He extended a hand and pulled the injured man to his feet.

Mertral nodded and he gestured at Dien. "I have found her, brother."

The newcomer turned to Dien then, and took a thunderous step, towering over her. He studied her, his sapphire eyes blazing.

Dien raised her bloody hammer, holding it as steady as she could. She was not yet certain if these winged men were friend or foe, and after winning her freedom at such a cost, she would not suffer thralldom ever again.

"Who are you?" Dien rasped.

"I am the Archangel Orphus. I come from Heaven."

Dien looked between the two-winged giants. None of what this newcomer said made sense. "I've never heard of Heaven. Is it south of the mountains?"

A moment's silence. "I have been sent by my father. He said we would find what we have been searching for here. His vision of our salvation." The angel's gaze pinned Dien. "Do you lead these people?"

Luci was the first to step up beside Dien. She had that blank look on her face again. Her black dagger dripped blood onto the smoking ground. Gartlen was next, balancing a sword too big for him on his shoulder. Samir staggered to his feet and wrenched the axe from Swordere's corpse. Karta stayed a few paces back, lazily twirling the sling at her side. Then, out of the smoke, came Arnut Poll, scarred Panyet, grumpy Narcy, and all the other thralls. All of them. Though they were thralls no more, Dien realised. Free men and women. Perhaps even the only free humans left in the world.

She turned back to the winged man, this Archangel. He was brilliant. So tall and imposing. He radiated power and strength. Dien found it a struggle to speak and her voice sounded small and ugly compared to his.

"You're the foe," she rasped, already knowing it was true. "The enemy the demons have been fighting."

The Archangel's armour creaked as he shifted and stared down at her. "We are no foe of yours, human, but we do fight the demons. Though, the war does not go well. We are outnumbered, sorely outmatched. We need allies. We need humanity to break the chains of thralldom that bind you and join us.

"My father sent me to find a leader to unite your people, and mine. He prophesied we would find our saviour here. Now." His armour clinked as he went down on one knee before her. His eyes burned with blue righteousness. "What is your name, human?"

Dien swallowed. Her mouth was horribly dry. "Dien Hostain."

The Archangel nodded, as if it suddenly all made sense. "Do you lead these people, Dien Hostain? Will you come to our aid? Free your people, unite us. Save us all."

Dien turned to look at the others. She'd been so ready to die, to sacrifice herself, not because she thought it was the only way to win them their freedom, but because she had nothing left to live for. Everything she had known, everyone she had loved had been stolen from her. But she had done it anyway. She had won them their freedom. Maybe that was something she could still live for: Helena's dream. For everyone. A life free of the demons, to choose for themselves.

"What do we do, Dien?" Luci asked.

Dien swept her eyes over them, met their gazes. Once villagers, then thralls, now free. Harder than they once were. Stronger. Forged like iron. What should they do? The answer seemed so obvious to her now. They would fight. And maybe, with these new winged allies, they could win.

She raised her hammer, still dripping with demon blood, above her head, and shouted, "On wings of vengeance and blood set ablaze, freedom for all mankind!"

AFTERWORD

Thank you so much for reading DEMON and I do hope you enjoyed the first adventure of a fledgeling Saint. If you did enjoy the book, please consider leaving a rating or review on Amazon, Goodreads, or any other platform you might frequent. Reviews are the lifeblood of books and you never know who you might inspire to give it a read.

And just a quick reminder that there are 2 companion trilogies being written alongside this one.

<u>The God Eater Saga</u> currently consists of:
Herald (Age of the God Eater #1)
Deathless (Annals of the God Eater #1)
Demon (Archive of the God Eater #1)

While each trilogy can be read on its own, the saga is designed to be consumed together to get the best picture of the world, the story, and the characters.

On wings of vengeance and blood set ablaze!

Rob

On wings of vengeance and blood set ablaze!

BOOKS BY ROB J. HAYES

The God Eater Saga (Heroic Epic Fantasy)

Herald (Age of the God Eater #1)

Deathless (Annals of the God Eater #1)

Demon (Archive of the God Eater #1)

The War Eternal (Dark Epic Fantasy)

Along the Razor's Edge

The Lessons Never Learned

From Cold Ashes Risen

Sins of the Mother

Death's Beating Heart

Titan Hoppers (Coming of Age Sci-Fantasy)

Titan Hoppers

Spire Climbers

The Mortal Techniques (Asian Sword & Sorcery)

Never Die

Pawn's Gambit

Spirits of Vengeance

The Century Blade (short story)

The First Earth Saga (Grimdark Fantasy)

The Heresy Within (The Ties that Bind #1)

The Colour of Vengeance (The Ties that Bind #2)

The Price of Faith (The Ties that Bind #3)

Where Loyalties Lie (Best Laid Plans #1)

The Fifth Empire of Man (Best Laid Plans #2)

City of Kings

<u>It Takes a Thief...</u> (Lighthearted Steampunk)

It Takes a Thief to Catch a Sunrise

It Takes a Thief to Start a Fire